alabaster
pale horse

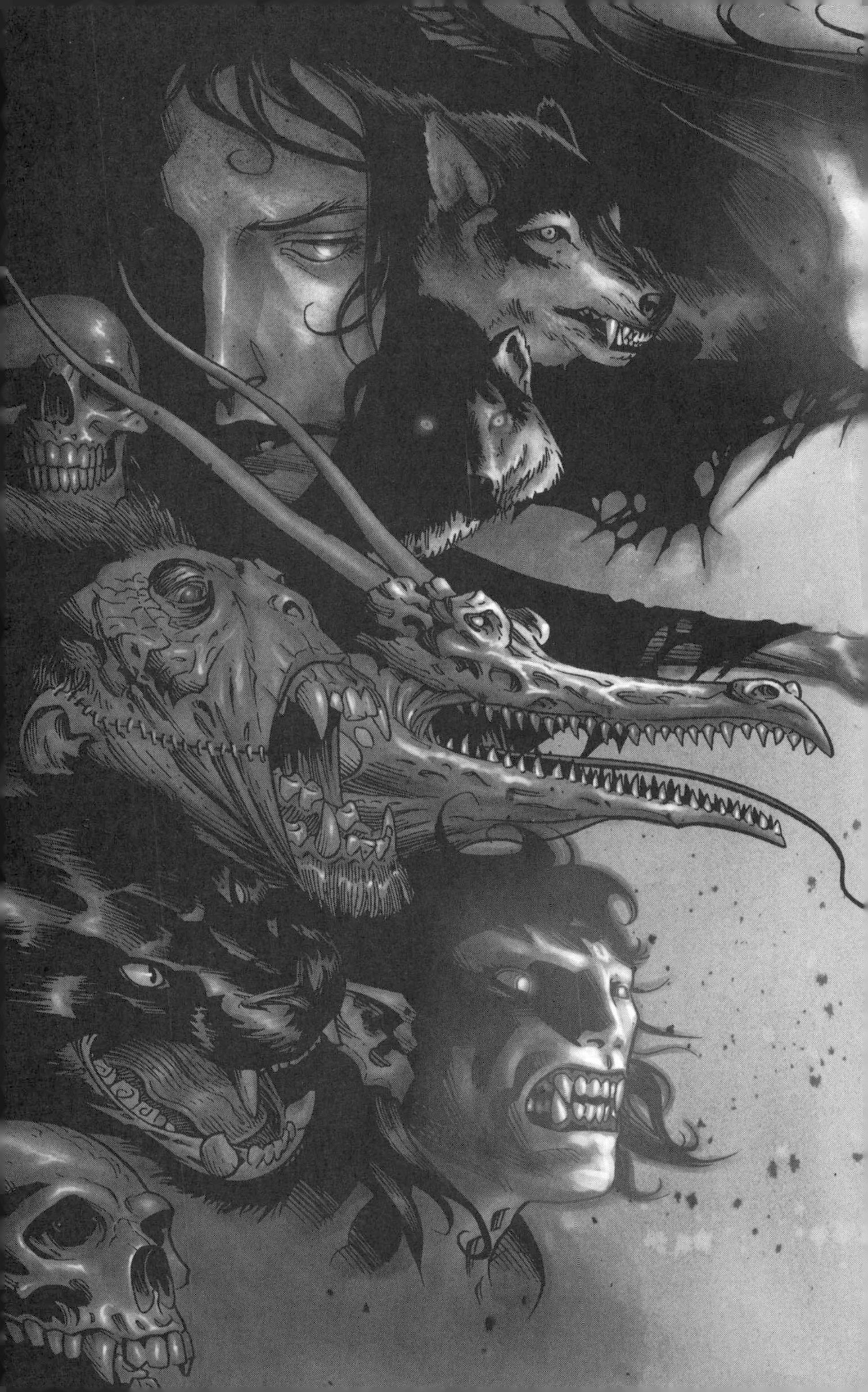

alabaster
pale horse

CAITLÍN R. KIERNAN

illustrations by Ted Naifeh

This volume collects short stories originally published in Caitlín R. Kiernan's *Alabaster* from Subterranean Press.

Cover design by Amy Arendts | Interior design by Krystal Randolph
Cover illustration by Greg Ruth

Published by Dark Horse Books
A division of Dark Horse Comics, Inc.
10956 SE Main Street
Milwaukie, OR 97222

DarkHorse.com
CaitlinrKiernan.com
ISBN 978-1-61655-300-5
First Dark Horse Books edition: February 2014

10 9 8 7 6 5 4 3 2 1
Printed in the United States of America

Library of Congress Cataloging-in-Publication Data

Kiernan, Caitlín R.
Alabaster : pale horse / Caitlín R. Kiernan ; illustrations by Ted Naifeh. -- First Dark Horse Books edition.
     pages cm
"This volume collects short stories originally published in Caitlín R. Kiernan's Alabaster from Far Territories"--Title page verso.
ISBN 978-1-61655-300-5
1. Young women--Fiction. 2. Albinos and albinism--Fiction. 3. Georgia--Fiction. I. Naifeh, Ted, illustrator. II. Title.
PS3561.I358A43 2014
813'.54--dc23
                                2013038460

Table of Contents

Stories by Chronological Order

The Well of Stars and Shadow
Highway 97
Bainbridge
Alabaster
Waycross
Les Fleurs Empoisonnées:
   or, Dans le Jardin des Fleurs Toxiques

Dedication

For Neil, and for Sophie, too.

In memory of Elizabeth Tillman Aldridge (1970–1995).

Preface

To date, I've written eleven novels and over two hundred short stories, and only a dozen or so times have I created a character who has intrigued me enough that I've returned to her or him. Dancy Flammarion is one of those characters.

This collection of short stories was first assembled and published in 2006, then reprinted in 2010, and, as you can see, both of those editions came with a preface. It speaks very well for the stories, so there's no reason to repeat it here. But something should be said about Dancy's transition from prose to comics and the differences between the two incarnations. Though, technically, there have been three incarnations of the character. I'll get to that.

In October 2010 I was in Portland, Oregon, as guest of honor at the annual H. P. Lovecraft Film Festival, and I was approached by Rachel Edidin, then an editor at Dark Horse Comics, who was interested in working with me on a project. Over the next few months, a number of ideas were tossed around, and finally I settled on a new Dancy Flammarion story. I'd not written one in five years, but I found it easier than I'd expected to return to her and her world, a sun-baked Deep South haunted by monsters and worse things than monsters. In the spring of 2011, I penned a short tale, "Bus Fare," for a future issue of *Dark Horse Presents*. And I thought that was it. No more Dancy. I went to work on another project, the next novel. But then Rachel approached me about adapting "Bus Fare" into comic script format, also for *Dark Horse Presents*. Cool, I said. Sure.

So, that's what I did. In June, I converted "Bus Fare" into a script.

And then, only a couple of weeks later, Rachel asked if I'd like to do a Dancy miniseries, using the "Bus Fare" script as the beginning of the story. And again I agreed. *Alabaster: Wolves* was born. The world glimpsed in the short story was fleshed out. Maisie and Bird became full-fledged characters, not merely foils for a beleaguered protagonist. Steve Lieber, Rachelle Rosenberg, and Greg Ruth came onboard, and together they made my words into pictures and brought Dancy Flammarion to life in a way I'd never expected she would be. The mini came to five issues and in 2013 appeared as a hardback graphic novel. This led to another, shorter series of Dancy stories, *Alabaster: Grimmer Tales* (originally *Alabaster: Boxcar Tales*), which appeared in the pages of *Dark Horse Presents* (#18–#22, #24, and #26–#32). Somewhere along the way, I began talking to Rachel and Mike Richardson about reissuing the short story collection, which had recently gone out of print. They agreed this was a good idea.

Greg Ruth's gorgeous cover for *Alabaster: Wolves* #5 would be used as the cover. And, voilà, a new edition of *Alabaster*, eight years after its initial appearance.

Now, a few notes on continuity.

Dancy was originally created for my second novel, *Threshold* (2001, Penguin/Roc/NAL). She was introduced to the world with these words: "The albino girl is reading *National Geographic* . . ." In the novel, Dancy is a sort of latter-day, southern gothic Joan of Arc, a sixteen-year-old on a crusade to destroy the otherworldly forces that destroyed her family. The book makes it plain that she's quite probably insane.

With the first Dancy Flammarion short story—"*Les Fleurs Empoisonnées*," suggested by a passage in the novel—I sort of rebooted the character. The series of events in the story didn't quite match up with that of *Threshold*. And with each successive story, *this* Dancy became less *that* Dancy. She became increasingly wiser and more world weary and less certain of herself. I think of the Dancy of the short stories as Dancy 2.0. When the stories were collected, Ted Naifeh gave her a face, creating the iconic incarnation of the character which has influenced all subsequent depictions.

When I approached *Alabaster: Wolves*, I knew I wanted a more mature version of Dancy Flammarion—one that wouldn't match up at all with the Dancy of *Threshold*. So, enter Dancy 3.0. Here she's much, much more world weary, and instead of besting every monster with relative ease, she tends to get her ass kicked in the process. Her victories come with terrible price tags. What was once, at least to her, a black-and-white world of good vs. evil, becomes profoundly gray. Indeed, a monster may turn out to be your best friend, a savior, someone who loves you. The miniseries also revisits part of the short stories "Alabaster" (my personal favorite) and "Bainbridge" and includes pretty much all of "Waycross." And once again, there's a completely new series of events, one that abandons the timeline and outcome of the short stories.

Dancy changed, because I'd changed as a writer. I never could have gone back to who she'd been at the start.

So, the Dancy Flammarion of the comics isn't quite the Dancy of the stories in this book. You'll soon see that. It's a different, and I think weirder, sort of trip than *Alabaster: Wolves* and *Alabaster: Grimmer Tales*.

This is the long, hot road Dancy walked *before* . . .

Caitlín R. Kiernan
18 September 2013
Providence, Rhode Island

Preface
to the First Edition

I cannot now recall where or when or why I first conceived of Dancy Flammarion. But then I can say the same thing about almost all of my characters, regardless of how fond of them I may (or may not) be. Almost inevitably, that moment when they initially occur to me is lost. Only later, after a story or two, after a novel or three, do those original thoughts take on any significance, and by then it's too late and I've forgotten. Hindsight's a bitch.

But the earliest mention of Dancy in my notes for *Threshold* is dated September 16, 1998. I describe her simply as a "creepy little 'Boo Radley' albino girl." Also, I know that I first came across the name Dancy that summer, while I was collecting fossils from the Upper Cretaceous of western Alabama. If you look at a map of the state—if you look very *closely*—you can probably find the "town" of Dancy on State Highway 17, a few miles east of the Mississippi state line in southern Pickens County. It had a post office, once upon a time, and might have been named for Dr. Edwin C. Dancy (b. 1810). I was there one blistering afternoon in July or August, and the name stuck in my head, as names often do, and so maybe it's fair to say *that's* where Dancy Flammarion began.

Now, more than eight years later, I've written four short stories and a novella about Dancy, though I'd genuinely never intended to go back to her after finishing with *Threshold*. But in the summer of 2001, while compiling material for *Trilobite: The*

Writing of Threshold, I was glancing through the novel and lingered on this passage from the end of chapter 8:

> This is the ravenous stone face that Dancy's dreamt of so many times, the same yawning, toothless mouth and those vacant, hollow eyes. Face of the thing that killed her mother and the vengeful ebony thing that came to take its body back into the swamp, the face of the smiling man from the Greyhound bus and the auburn-haired woman in Waycross with stubby, writhing tentacles where her breasts should have been, the pretty boy in Savannah who showed her a corked amber bottle that held three thousand ways to suffer, three thousand ways to hurt, before she killed him. All of them dead because that's what the angel said, and she's standing here holding tight to these iron bars so she doesn't fall, too weak to stand and the mountain looming above her, because this is where the angel said she had to go. (page 134)

Suddenly, I wanted to tell one of these stories. Specifically, I wanted to know exactly what had happened to Dancy in Savannah when she met the pretty boy with the deadly amber bottle, and I began work on a story called "*Les Fleurs Empoisonnées*," which I intended to include in the chapbook. But then it proved to be a rather longish story, and Bill Schafer at Subterranean Press proposed it be published on its own as a small hardback. I asked if I could get Dame Darcy to illustrate it, as one of her drawings had been a very important inspiration, and he said sure, but would I change the title to something that wasn't French. I agreed, and "*Les Fleurs Empoisonnées*" was released as *In the Garden of Poisonous Flowers* in March 2002. We were even able to use the Dame Darcy piece that had given me the ghoulish women of the Stephens Ward Tea League and Society of Resurrectionists for the book's endpapers.

And, as it turned out, by the time *In the Garden of Poisonous Flowers* was in print, I'd already written a second Dancy story, a strange little piece about her childhood in the swamps of Okaloosa County, Florida. Titled "The Well of Stars and Shadow," it was written at the very tail end of October 2001 (thank you, Spooky) and appeared first on Gothic.net on the twelfth of that November. It was also included in *Trilobite: The Writing of Threshold* (which, for one reason and another, wasn't released until 2003). Only a few months later, in March 2002, I wrote my third Dancy short story, "Waycross," which was released as a chapbook by Subterranean Press, beautifully illustrated by Ted Naifeh (those four illustrations are reprinted herein). Like *"Les Fleurs Empoisonnées"* before it, "Waycross" grew out of that paragraph from the end of chapter 8 of *Threshold*, elucidating another of the episodes I'd begun to wonder about. In August, as I was finishing with *Low Red Moon*, I wrote in my online journal (9/17/02), "I know I still have one more Dancy story left to write, a prequel to 'Waycross,' but it may be months before I have time to write it." I suspected it would be titled "Bainbridge," and by this time Bill Schafer was asking about doing a collection of Dancy stories.

But then on March 18, 2003, roughly a year after I'd written "Waycross," I wrote an unanticipated piece called "Alabaster." Again, I refer to an entry from my online journal (these things can be very convenient): "I did something I've never done before. I conceived of *and* finished a short story on the same day. I'd never even begun and finished a short story on the same day before. It's a very short piece, only about 1,000 words, for the Camelot 'chapette' book, titled 'Alabaster.' A brief glimpse at Dancy Flammarion on her way to 'Waycross,' set before that story, *Threshold*, and *In the Garden of Poisonous Flowers*." In 2004, as I began to plan for the Dancy collection, I expanded

"Alabaster" into a full-length short story, which appears in print for the first time in this collection.

The final short story in this book, "Bainbridge," which I believe will be the last time I write about Dancy, was begun in December 2005 and completed just after the New Year. I'm not going to say much more about it, as it has a few surprises (I know they surprised me) which I don't want to spoil. Among other things, the story deals with Dancy's mother, Julia Flammarion, and her attempt to drown herself off Pensacola Beach in December 1982.

Also the reader will note that, as with *Tales of Pain and Wonder*, I have provided the reader with a second table of contents, for those who wish to read the stories in chronological order rather than the order in which they were written (my personal preference).

It seems as though I ought to have more to say here, something more substantial than this simple litany of dates. Dancy has been in my head for a long, long time now. I've returned to her again and again. The word *avatar* comes to mind, and its original Sanskrit meaning—the incarnation of a god in animal or human form. Dancy has certainly been that, though I think I'll leave the reader to draw his or her own conclusions about the ultimate nature of the god or gods that Dancy Flammarion might be made *incarnate*. And, of course, Dancy has also served as an avatar for some dark splinter of my own being, the incarnation of my own seemingly bottomless fury at the world around me, the splinter which wants no part of tedious Reason and Compromise, the angry, seething splinter that would be a lot happier addressing this or that perceived injustice with a carving knife than settling for mere words. There's a paradox here, of course. While I doubt I'm quite monstrous enough to ever show up on Dancy's hit list, I'm also pretty sure she'd have about as much use for me as she did for those wicked Ladies in

Savannah. That doesn't make me love her any less, though. Like the Gynander and Sinethella, I have no illusions about my own monstrosity. It only makes it harder for me to consider the trials I've seen fit to visit upon Dancy.

I think this is all about mirrors, more than anything else, mirrors and lost innocence. I think it's also about the terrible consequences of misguided belief. And insanity. And there's still something *more*, something I can't quite seem to get at, like a last bit of marrow in some inconvenient crevice of a shattered bone. Maybe you'll see it for yourselves, or maybe I'm only jumping at shadows.

My thanks to Bill Schafer, because I never would have written this book without his enthusiasm and encouragement. And to Spooky, who hides the knives from me. And to my agent, Merrilee Heifetz. A big thank-you to Ted Naifeh for making much more of this book than my words, and to Dame Darcy, for inspiration and for her work on *In the Garden of Poisonous Flowers*. And I'm sure there are other people who should be thanked. There always are. But now it's time to start the show. Someone get the lights . . .

Caitlín R. Kiernan
16 January 2006
Atlanta, Georgia

. . . abasht the Devil stood,
And felt how awful goodness is . . .
John Milton, *Paradise Lost*

Every angel is terrifying.
Rainer Maria Rilke, *Duino Elegies*

Les Fleurs Empoisonnées:
or, Dans le Jardin des Fleurs Toxiques

Miles past a town named Vidalia, town named after an onion, onion named after a town, but Dead Girl has no idea how many miles, the vast, unremarkable Georgia night like a seamless quilt of stars and kudzu vines and all these roads look the same to her. The Bailiff behind the wheel of the rusty black Monte Carlo they picked up in Jacksonville after the Oldsmobile broke down, Bobby in the front seat beside him, playing with the dials on the radio; the endless chain of honky-tonk and gospel stations is broken only by the spit and crackle of static squeezed in between. Dead Girl's alone in the back seat reading one of her books by moonlight. She asks Bobby to stop, please, because he's getting on her nerves, probably getting on the Bailiff's nerves, too. He pauses long enough to glance back at her, and his silver eyes flash like mercury and rainwater coins. He might be any six-year-old boy, except for those eyes.

"Let him be," the Bailiff says. "He isn't bothering me." Bobby smirks at her, sticks out his tongue, and goes back to playing with the radio.

"Suit yourself," Dead Girl says and turns a page, even though she hasn't finished reading the last one.

"Well, well, now," the Bailiff says and he laughs his husky, dry-wheeze laugh. "*There's* a sight . . ."

And the Monte Carlo's brakes squeal, metal grinding metal, and the car drifts off the road. Dead Girl sits up, and she can see the hitchhiker in the headlights, a teenage girl holding up one hand to shield her eyes from the glare.

"I'm not hungry," Bobby says as if someone had asked, and Dead Girl stares at the Bailiff's reflection in the rearview mirror. But there's no explanation waiting for her in his green eyes, his easy smile, the secretive parchment creases of his ancient face; she wishes for the hundredth time that she'd stayed in Providence with Gable, better things to do than riding around the sticks picking up runaways and bums. Having to sleep in the trunks of rattletrap automobiles while the Bailiff runs his errands beneath the blazing Southern sun, sun so bright and violent that even the night seems scorched.

"Maybe this one ain't for eating, boy," the Bailiff chuckles, and the Monte Carlo rolls to a stop in a cloud of dust and grit and carbon monoxide. "Maybe this one's something you've never seen before."

The girl's wearing dark wraparound sunglasses, and her hair is as white as milk, milk spun into the finest silken thread, talcum-powder skin, and "It's just an albino," Dead Girl mutters, disappointed. "You think we've never seen an albino before?"

The Bailiff laughs again and honks the horn. The girl leans forward and squints at them through her sunglasses and the settling dust, takes a hesitant step towards the car. She's wearing a faded yellow Minnie Mouse T-shirt and carrying a tattered duffel bag.

"Pure as the driven snow, this one here. Funeral lilies and barbed wire. Keep your eyes open, both of you, or she just might teach you something you don't want to learn."

"Christ," Dead Girl hisses and slumps back in her seat. "I thought we were in such a big, damn hurry. I thought Miss Aramat was—"

"Watch your tongue, child," the Bailiff growls back, and now his eyes flash angry emerald fire at her from the rearview mirror. "Mind your *place*," and then Bobby's rolling down his window, and the albino girl peers doubtfully into the Monte Carlo.

"Where you bound, sister?" the Bailiff asks, and she doesn't answer right away, looks warily at Bobby and Dead Girl and then back at the road stretching away into the summer night.

"Savannah," the albino girl says, finally. "I'm on my way to Savannah," and Dead Girl can hear the misgiving, the guarded apprehension, weighting the edges of her voice.

"Well, now, how about that. Would you believe we're headed that way ourselves? Don't just sit there, Bobby. Open the door for the girl and help her with that bag—"

"Maybe I should wait on the next car," she says and wrinkles her nose like a rabbit. "There's already three of you. There might not be enough room."

"Nonsense," the Bailiff replies. "There's plenty of room, isn't there, children?" Bobby opens his door and takes her duffel bag, stuffs it into the floorboard behind his seat. The albino looks at the road one more time, and for a moment Dead Girl thinks maybe she's going to run, wonders if the Bailiff will chase her if she does, if it's *that* sort of lesson.

"Thanks," she says, sounding anything but grateful, and climbs into the back and sits beside Dead Girl. Bobby slams his door shut, and the Monte Carlo's tires spin uselessly for a moment, flinging up sand and gravel, before they find traction and the car lurches forward onto the road.

"You from Vidalia?" the Bailiff asks, and the girl nods her head, but doesn't say anything. Dead Girl closes her book— *Charlotte's Web* in Latin, *Tela Charlottae*—and lays it on the seat between them. The albino smells like old sweat and dirty clothes, like fresh air and the warm blood in her veins. Bobby turns around in his seat and watches her with curious silver eyes.

"What's her name?" he asks Dead Girl, and the Bailiff swerves to miss something lying in the road.

"Dancy," the albino says. "Dancy Flammarion," and she takes off her sunglasses, reveals eyes the deep red-pink of pyrope or the pulpy hearts of fresh strawberries.

"Is she blind?" Bobby asks, and "How the hell would I know?" Dead Girl grumbles. "Ask her yourself."

"Are you blind?"

"No," Dancy tells him, the hard edge in her voice to say she knows this is a game, a taunting formality, and maybe she's seen it all before. "But the light hurts my eyes."

"Mine, too," Bobby says.

"Oculocutaneous albinism," the Bailiff chimes in. "A genetic defect in the body's ability to convert the amino acid tyrosine into melanin. Ah, but we're being rude, Bobby. She probably doesn't like to talk about it."

"No, that's all right. It doesn't bother me," and Dancy leans suddenly, boldly, forward, leaving only inches between herself and Bobby. The movement surprises him, and he jumps.

"What about *you*, Bobby? What's wrong with *your* eyes?" Dancy asks him.

"I—" he begins and then pauses and looks uncertainly at Dead Girl and the Bailiff. Dead Girl shrugs, no idea what the rules in this charade might be, and the Bailiff keeps his eyes on the road.

"That's okay," Dancy says, and she winks at him. "You don't have to tell me if you don't want to, if you're not supposed to tell. The angel tells me what I need to know."

"*You* have an angel?" and now Bobby sounds skeptical.

"Everyone has an angel. Well, everyone I ever met so far. Even you, Bobby. Didn't they tell you that?"

Dead Girl sighs and picks her book up again, opens it to a page she's read twice already.

"Why don't you see if you can find something on the radio," she says to Bobby.

"But I'm still talking to Dancy."

"You'll have plenty of time to talk to Dancy, boy," the Bailiff says. "She isn't going anywhere."

"She's going to Savannah with us."

"Except Savannah," Dancy says very softly, faint smile at the corners of her mouth, and she turns away and looks out the window at the night-shrouded fields and farmhouses rushing silently past. Bobby stares at her for another minute or two, like he's afraid she might disappear, then he goes back to playing with the radio knobs.

"You too, Mercy Brown," the albino whispers, and Dead Girl stops reading.

"*What?*" she asks. "What did you just say to me?"

"I dreamed about you once, Mercy. I dreamed about you sleeping at the bottom of a cold river, crabs tangled in your hair and this boy in your arms." Dancy keeps her eyes on the window as she talks, her voice so cool, so unafraid, like maybe she climbs into cars with demons every goddamn night of the week.

"I dreamed about you and snow. You got an angel, too."

"*You* shut the fuck up," Dead Girl snarls. "That's not my name, and I don't care *who* you are, you shut up or—"

"You'll kill me anyway," Dancy says calmly, "so what's the difference?" and up front the Bailiff chuckles to himself. Bobby finds a station playing an old Johnny Cash song, "The Reverend Mr. Black," and he sings along.

Southeast and the land turns from open prairie and piney woods to salt marsh and estuaries, confluence of muddy, winding rivers, blackwater piss of the distant Appalachians, the Piedmont hills, and everything between. The low country, *no fayrer or fytter place*, all cordgrass and wax myrtle, herons and crayfish, and the old city laid out wide and flat where the Savannah River runs finally into the patient, hungry sea. The end of Sherman's March, and this swampy gem spared the Yankee torches, saved by gracious women and their soirée seductions, and in 1864 the whole city made a grand Christmas gift to Abraham Lincoln.

The mansion on East Hall Street, Stephens Ward, built seventeen long years later, Reconstruction days, and Mr. Theodosius W. Ybanes hired a fashionable architect from Rhode Island to design his eclectic, mismatched palace of masonry and wrought iron, Gothic pilasters and high Italianate balconies. The mansard roof tacked on following a hurricane in 1888 and, after Theodosius's death, the house handed down to his children and grandchildren, great-grandchildren, generations come and gone and, unlike most of Savannah's stately old homes, this house has never passed from the direct bloodline of its first master.

And, at last, delivered across the decades, a furious red century and decades more, into the small, slender hands of Miss Aramat Drawdes, great-great-great-granddaughter of a Civil War munitions merchant and unspoken matriarch of the Stephens Ward Tea League and Society of Resurrectionists. The first female descendant of Old Ybanes not to take a husband, her sexual, social, and culinary proclivities entirely too unorthodox to permit even a marriage of convenience, but Miss Aramat keeps her own sort of family in the rambling mansion on East Hall Street. Behind yellow, glazed-brick walls, azaleas and ivy, windows blinded by heavy drapes, the house keeps its own counsel, its own world apart from the prosaic customs and concerns of the city.

And from appearances, this particular night in June is nothing special, not like the time they found the transsexual junkie who'd hung herself with baling wire in Forsyth Park, or last October, when Candida had the idea of carving all their jack-o'-lanterns from human and ape skulls and then setting them out on the porches in plain sight. Nothing so unusual or extravagant, only the traditional Saturday night indulgences: the nine Ladies of the League and Society (nine now, but there have been more and less, at other times), assembled in the Yellow Room. Antique velvet wallpaper the pungent color of saffron, and they sit, or stand, or lie outstretched on the Turkish carpet, the cushions strewn about the floor and a couple of threadbare recamiers. Miss Aramat and her eight exquisite sisters, the nine who would be proper ghouls if only they'd been born to better skins than these fallible, ephemeral husks. They paint their lips like open wounds, their eyes like bruises. Their fine dresses are not reproductions, every gown and corset and crinoline vintage Victorian or Edwardian, and never anything later than 1914, because that's the year the world ended, Miss Aramat says.

A lump of sticky black opium in the tall, octopean hookah and there are bottles of burgundy, pear brandy, chartreuse, and cognac, but tonight Miss Aramat prefers the bitter Spanish absinthe, and she watches lazily as Isolde balances a slotted silver trowel on the rim of her glass. A single sugar cube, and the girl pours water from a carafe over the trowel, dissolving the sugar, drip, drip, drip, and the liqueur turns the milky green of polished jade.

"Me next," Emily demands from her seat on one of the yellow recamiers, but Isolde ignores her, pours herself an absinthe and sits on the floor at Miss Aramat's bare feet. She smirks at Emily, who rolls her blue, exasperated eyes and reaches for the brandy, instead.

"Better watch yourself, Isolde," Biancabella warns playfully from her place beneath a Tiffany floor lamp, stained-glass light like shattered sunflowers to spill across her face and shoulders. "One day we're gonna have *your* carcass on the table."

"In your dreams," Isolde snaps back, but she nestles in deeper between Miss Aramat's legs, anyway, takes refuge in the protective cocoon of her stockings and petticoat, the folds of her skirt.

Later, of course, there will be dinner, the mahogany sideboard in the dining room laid out with sweetbreads *de champignon*, boiled terrapin lightly flavored with nutmeg and sherry, yams and okra and red rice, raw oysters, Jerusalem artichokes, and a dozen desserts to choose from. Then Alma and Biancabella will play for them, cello and violin, until it's time to go down to the basement and the evening's anatomizing.

Madeleine turns another card, the Queen of Cups, and Porcelina frowns, not exactly what she was hoping for, already growing bored with Maddy's dry prognostications; she looks over her left shoulder at Miss Aramat.

"I saw Samuel again this week," she says. "He told me the bottle has started to sing at night, if the moon's bright enough."

Miss Aramat stops running her fingers through Isolde's curly blonde hair and stares silently at Porcelina for a moment. Another sip of absinthe, sugar and anise on her tongue, and "I thought we had an understanding," she says. "I thought I'd asked you not to mention him ever again, not in my presence, not in this house."

Porcelina glances back down at the tarot card, pushes her violet-tinted pince-nez farther up the bridge of her nose.

"He says that the Jamaicans are offering him a lot of money for it."

Across the room, Candida stops reading to Mary Rose, closes the copy of *Unaussprechlichen Kulten*, and glares at Porcelina. "You may be the youngest," she says. "But that's no excuse for impudence. You were *told*—"

"But I've *seen* it, with my own eyes I've seen it," and now she doesn't sound so bold, not half so confident as only an instant before. Madeleine is trying to ignore the whole affair, gathers up her deck and shuffles the cards.

"You've seen what he wants you to see. What he *made* you see," Miss Aramat says. "Nothing more. The bottle's a fairy tale, and Samuel and the rest of those old conjurers know damn well that's all it will ever be."

"But what if it isn't? What if just one *half* the things he says are true?"

"Drop it," Candida mutters and opens her book again.

"Yes," Mary Rose says. "We're all sick to death of hearing about Samuel and that goddamn bottle."

But Miss Aramat keeps her bottomless hazel-green eyes on Porcelina, takes another small swallow of absinthe. She tangles her fingers in Isolde's hair and pulls her head back sharply, exposing the girl's pale throat to the room; they can all see the scars, the puckered worm-pink slashes between Isolde's pretty chin and her high lace collar.

"Then you go and call him, Porcelina," Miss Aramat says very softly. "Tell him to bring the bottle here, tonight. Tell him I want a demonstration."

Madeleine stops shuffling her cards, and Biancabella reaches for the brandy, even though her glass isn't empty.

"Before four o'clock, tell him, but after three. I don't want him or one of his little boys interrupting the formalities."

And when she's absolutely certain that Miss Aramat has finished, when Isolde has finally been allowed to lower her chin and hide the scars, Porcelina stands up and goes alone to the telephone in the hallway.

In the basement of the house on East Hall Street there are three marble embalming tables laid end to end beneath a row of fluorescent lights. The lights one of Miss Aramat's few, grudging concessions to modernity, though for a time they worked only by candlelight, and then incandescent bulbs strung above the tables. But her eyes aren't what they used to be, and there was Biancabella's astigmatism to consider, as well. So she bought the fluorescents in a government auction at Travis Field, and now every corner of the basement is bathed in stark white light, clinical light to illuminate the most secret recesses of their subjects.

Moldering red-brick walls, and here and there the sandy, earthen floor has been covered with sheets of varnished plywood, a makeshift, patchwork walkway so their boots don't get too muddy whenever it rains. An assortment of old cabinets and shelves lines the walls, bookshelves and glass-fronted display cases; at least a thousand stoppered apothecary bottles, specimen jars of various shapes and sizes filled with ethyl alcohol or formalin to preserve the ragged things and bits of things that float inside. Antique microscopes, magnifying lenses, and prosthetic limbs, a human skeleton dangling from a hook screwed into the roof of its yellowed skull, each bone carefully labeled with India ink in Miss Aramat's spidery hand.

Alma's collection of aborted and pathologic fetuses occupies the entire northwest corner of the basement, and another corner has been given over to Mary Rose's obsession with the cranium of *Homo sapiens*. So far, she has fifty-three (including the dozen or so sacrificed for Candida's jack-o'-lanterns), classified as Negroid, Australoid, Mongoloid, and Xanthochroid, according to T. H. Huxley's 1870 treatise on the races of man. Opposite the embalming tables is a long, low counter of carved and polished oak—half funereal shrine, half laboratory workbench— where Emily's framed photographs of deceased members of the League and Society, lovingly adorned with personal mementos and bouquets of dried flowers, vie for space with Madeleine's jumble of beakers, test tubes, and bell jars.

Nearer the stairs, there's a great black double-door safe that none of them has ever tried to open, gold filigree and L. H. MILLER SAFE AND IRONWORKS, BALTIMORE, M.D. painted on one door just above the brass combination dial. Long ago, before Miss Aramat was born, someone stored a portrait of an elderly woman in a blue dress atop the safe, anonymous, unframed canvas propped against the wall, and the years and constant damp have taken their toll. The painting has several large holes, the handiwork of insects and fungi, and the woman's features have been all but obliterated.

"I've never even *heard* of a Skithian," Isolde says, reaching behind her back to tie the strings of her apron.

"*Scy*thian, dear," Miss Aramat corrects her. "S-c-y, like *scythe*, but the *c* and *y* make a short *i* instead of a long *i*."

"Oh," Isolde says and yawns. "Well, I've never heard of *them*, either," and she watches as Biancabella makes the first cut, drawing her scalpel expertly between the small breasts of the woman lying on the middle table. Following the undertaker's original Y incision, she slices cleanly through the sutures that hold the corpse's torso closed.

"An ancient people who probably originated in Anatolia and northern Mesopotamia," Biancabella says as she carefully traces the line of stitches. "Their kingdom was conquered by the Iranian Sarmatians, and by the early sixth century BC they'd mostly become nomads wandering the Kuban, and later the Pontic steppes—"

Isolde yawns again, louder than before, loud enough to interrupt Biancabella. "You sound like a teacher I had in high school. He always smelled like mentholated cough drops."

"They might have *been* Iranian," Madeleine says. "I know I read that somewhere."

Biancabella sighs and stops cutting the sutures, her blade lingering an inch or so above the dead woman's navel, and she glares up at Madeleine.

"They were *not* Iranian. Haven't you even bothered to read Plinius?" she asks and points the scalpel at Madeleine. " '*Ultra sunt Scytharum populi, Persae illos Sacas in universum applelavere a proxima gente, antiqui Arameos.*' "

"Where the hell is Arameos?" Madeleine asks, cocking one eyebrow suspiciously.

"Northern Mesopotamia."

"Who cares?" Isolde mumbles, and Biancabella shakes her head in disgust and goes back to work. "Obviously, some more than others," she says.

Miss Aramat reaches for the half-empty bottle of wine that Mary Rose has left on the table near the corpse's knees. She takes a long swallow of the burgundy, wipes her mouth across the back of her hand, smearing her lipstick slightly. "According to Herodotus, the Scythians disemboweled their dead kings," she says and passes the bottle to Isolde. "Then they stuffed the abdominal cavity with cypress, parsley seed, frankincense, and anise. Afterwards, the body was sewn shut again and entirely covered with wax."

Biancabella finishes with the sutures, lays aside her scalpel and uses both hands to force open the dead woman's belly. The sweet, caustic smells of embalming fluid and rot, already palpable in the stagnant basement air, seem to rise like steam from the interior of the corpse.

"Of course, we don't have the parsley *seed*," she says and glances across the table at Porcelina, "because someone's Greek isn't exactly what it ought to be."

"It's close enough," Porcelina says defensively, and she points an index finger at the bowl of fresh, chopped parsley lined up with all the other ingredients for the ritual. "I can't imagine that Miss Whoever She Might Be here's going to give a damn one way or another."

Biancabella begins inserting her steel dissection hooks through the stiffened flesh at the edges of the incision, each hook attached to a slender chain fastened securely to the rafters overhead. "Will someone please remind me again why we took this little quim in?"

"Well, she's a damn good fuck," Madeleine says. "At least when she's sober."

"And she makes a mean corn pudding," Alma adds.

"Oh, yes. The corn pudding. How could I have possibly forgotten the corn pudding."

"Next time," Porcelina growls, "you can fucking do it yourselves."

"No, dear," Miss Aramat says, her voice smooth as the tabletop, cold as the heart of the dead woman. "Next time, you'll do it right. Or there may not be another time after that."

Porcelina turns her back on them, then, turning because she's afraid they might see straight through her eyes to the hurt and doubt coiled about her soul. She stares instead at the louvered window above Mary Rose's skulls, the glass painted black, shiny, thick black latex to stop the day and snooping eyes.

"Well, you have to admit, at least then we'd never have to hear about that fucking bottle again," Candida laughs, and, as though her laughter were an incantation, skillful magic to shatter the moment, the back doorbell rings directly overhead. A buzz like angry, electric wasps filtered through the floorboards, and Miss Aramat looks at Porcelina, who hasn't taken her eyes off the window.

"You told him three o'clock?" Miss Aramat asks.

"I *told* him," Porcelina replies, sounding scared, and Miss Aramat nods her head once, takes off her apron, and returns it to a bracket on the wall.

"If I need you, I'll call," she says to Biancabella, and, taking what remains of the burgundy, goes upstairs to answer the door.

"Maybe Bobby and me should stay with the car," Dead Girl says again, in case the Bailiff didn't hear her the first time. Big, blustery man fiddling with his keys, searching for the one that fits the padlock on the iron gate; he stops long enough to glance back at her and shake his head *no*. The moonlight glints dull off his bald scalp, and he scratches at his beard and glares at the uncooperative keys.

"But I saw a cop back there," Dead Girl says. "What if he finds the car and runs the plates? What if—"

"We can always get another car," the Bailiff grumbles. "Better he finds a stolen car than a stolen car with the two of you sitting inside."

"And I wanna see the Ladies," Bobby chirps, swings the Bailiff's leather satchel, and Dead Girl wishes she could smack him, would if the Bailiff weren't standing right there to see her do it.

Bobby leans close to the albino girl and stands on tiptoes, his lips pressed somewhere below her left ear. There's a piece of duct tape across her mouth, silver duct tape wrapped tight around her wrists, and Dead Girl's holding onto the collar of her Minnie Mouse T-shirt. "They're like *ghouls*," he whispers, "only nicer."

"No, they're not," Dead Girl snorts. "Not real ghouls. Real ghouls don't live in great big fucking houses."

"You'll see," Bobby whispers to Dancy. "They dig up dead people and cut them into pieces. That's what ghouls do."

And the Bailiff finds the right key, then—"*There* you are, my rusty little sparrow"—and the hasp pops open and in a moment they're through the gate and standing in the garden. Dead Girl looks longingly back at the alleyway and the Monte Carlo as the Bailiff pulls the gate shut behind him, *clang*, and snaps the padlock closed again.

The garden is darker than the alley, the low, sprawling limbs of live oaks and magnolias to hide the moon, crooked limbs draped with Spanish moss and epiphytic ferns. Dancy has to squint to see. She draws a deep breath through her nostrils, taking in the sticky, flower-scented night, camellias and boxwood, the fleshy white magnolia blossoms. Behind her, the Bailiff's keys jangle, and Dead Girl shoves Dancy roughly forward, towards the house.

The Bailiff leads the way down the narrow cobblestone path that winds between the trees, past a brass sundial and marble statues set on marble pedestals, nude bodies wrapped in shadow garments, unseeing stone eyes staring after Heaven. Dancy counts her steps, listens to the Bailiff's fat-man wheeze, the twin silences where Dead Girl and Bobby's breath should be. Only the slightest warm breeze to disturb the leaves, the drone of crickets and katydids, and, somewhere nearby, a whippoorwill calling out to other whippoorwills.

A thick hedge of oleander bushes, and then the path turns abruptly and they're standing at the edge of a reflecting pool choked with hyacinth and water lilies; broad flagstones to ring its dark circumference, and the Bailiff pauses here, stares down at the water, and rubs his beard. An expression on his face like someone who's lost something, someone who knows he'll never find it again, or it'll never find him.

"What is it?" Dead Girl asks. "What's wrong?" but the Bailiff only shrugs his broad shoulders, and takes another step nearer the pool, standing right at the very edge now.

"One day," he says. "One day, when you're older, maybe, I'll tell you about this place. One day maybe I'll even tell you what she keeps trapped down there at the bottom with the goldfish and the tadpoles."

He laughs, an ugly, bitter sound, and Dancy makes herself turn away from the pool. She can hear the drowned things muttering to themselves below the surface, even if Dead Girl can't, the rheumy voices twined with roots and slime. She looks up at the house instead and sees they've almost reached the steps leading to the high back porch. Some of the downstairs windows glow with soft yellow light, light that can't help but seem inviting after so much darkness. But Dancy knows better, knows a lie when she sees one, and there's nothing to comfort or save her behind those walls. She takes another deep breath and starts walking towards the steps before Dead Girl decides to shove her again.

"You still got that satchel?" the Bailiff asks, and "Yes sir," the boy with silver eyes answers and holds it up so he can see. "It's getting heavy."

"Well, you just hang in there, boy. It's going to be getting a whole lot lighter any minute now."

And they climb the stairs together, Dancy in the lead, still counting the paces, the Bailiff at the rear, and the wooden steps creak loudly beneath their feet. At the top, the Bailiff presses the doorbell, and Dead Girl pushes Dancy into an old wicker chair.

"Where's your angel now?" she sneers and digs her sharp nails into the back of Dancy's neck and forces her head down between her knees.

"Be careful, child," the Bailiff says. "Don't start asking questions you don't really want answered," and now he's staring back towards the alley, across the wide, wide garden towards the car. "She might show you an angel or two, before this night's done."

And Dead Girl opens her mouth to tell him to fuck off and never mind her "place" because babysitting deranged albino girls was never part of the deal. But the back door opens then, light spilling from the house, and Dead Girl and Bobby both cover their eyes and look away. Dancy raises her head, wishing they hadn't taken her sunglasses, and she strains to see more than the silhouette of the woman standing in the doorway.

"Well, isn't this a surprise," the woman says, and then she leads them all inside.

Through the bright kitchen and down a long, dimly lit hall, walls hung with gilt-framed paintings of scenes that might have found their way out of Dancy's own nightmares. Midnight cemetery pictures, opened graves and broken headstones, a riot of hunched and prancing figures, dog-jawed, fire-eyed creatures, dragging corpses from the desecrated earth.

"We can have our tea in the Crimson Room," the woman named Miss Aramat says to the Bailiff. Small woman barely as tall as Dancy, china-doll hands and face, china-doll clothes, and Dancy thinks she might shatter if she fell, if anyone ever struck her. The jewels about her throat sparkle like drops of blood and morning dew set in silver, and she's wearing a big black hat, broad brimmed and tied with bunches of lace and ribbon, two iridescent peacock feathers stuck in the band. Her waist cinched so small that Dancy imagines one hand would reach almost all the way around it, thumb to middle finger. She isn't old, though Dancy wouldn't exactly call her a young woman, either.

Miss Aramat opens a door and ushers them into a room the color of a slaughterhouse: red walls, red floors, crossed swords above a red-tiled fireplace, a stuffed black bear wearing a red fez standing guard in one corner. She tugs on a braided bell pull and somewhere deep inside the house there's the muffled sound of chimes.

"I didn't expect you until tomorrow night," she says to the Bailiff and motions for him to take a seat in an armchair upholstered with cranberry brocade.

"Jacksonville took less time than I'd expected," he replies, shifting his weight about, trying to find a comfortable way to sit in an uncomfortable chair. "You seemed anxious to get this shipment. I trust we're not intruding—"

"Oh, no, no," Miss Aramat says. "Of course not," and she smiles a smile that makes Dancy think of an alligator.

"Well, this time I have almost everything you asked for," and then the armchair cracks loudly, and he stops fidgeting and sits still, glances apologetically at Miss Aramat. "Except the book. I'm afraid my man on Magazine Street didn't come through on that count."

"Ah. I'm sorry to hear that. Biancabella will be disappointed."

"However," the Bailiff says quickly and jabs a pudgy thumb towards Dancy, who's sitting now between Dead Girl and Bobby on a long red sofa. "I think perhaps I have something here that's going to more than make up for it."

And Miss Aramat pretends she hasn't already noticed Dancy, that she hasn't been staring at her for the last five minutes. "That's marvelous," she says, though Dancy catches the doubtful edge in her voice, the hesitation. "I don't think we've ever had an albino before."

"Oh, she's not just any albino," the Bailiff says, grins, and scratches his beard. "You must have heard about the unpleasantness in Waycross last month. Well, *this* is the girl who did the killing."

And something passes swiftly across Miss Aramat's face, then, a fleeting wash of fear or indignation, and she takes a step back towards the doorway.

"My God, man. And you brought her *here*?"

"Don't worry. I think she's actually quite harmless."

The Bailiff winks at Dead Girl, and she slams an elbow into Dancy's ribs to prove his point. Her breath rushes out through her nostrils and she doubles over, gasping uselessly against the duct tape still covering her mouth. A sickening swirl of black and purple fireflies dances before her eyes.

I'm going to throw up, she thinks. *I'm going to throw up and choke to death.*

"You ask me, someone must be getting sloppy down there in Waycross," the Bailiff says, "if this skinny little one could do that much damage. Anyway, when we found her, I thought to myself, now who would appreciate such an extraordinary morsel as this, such a tender pink delicacy?"

Miss Aramat is chewing indecisively at a thumbnail, and she tugs the bell pull again, harder this time, impatient, stomps the floor twice, and "No extra charge?" she asks.

"Not a penny. You'll be doing us all a favor."

Dancy shuts her eyes tight, breathing through her nose, tasting blood and bile at the back of her mouth. The Bailiff and Miss Aramat are still talking, but their voices seem far away now, inconsequential. This is the house where she's going to die, and she doesn't understand why the angel never told her that. The night in Waycross when she drove her knife into the heart of a monster dressed in the skins of dead men and animals, or before that, the one she killed in Bainbridge. Each time the angel was there to tell her it was right, the world a cleaner place for her work, but never a word about this house and the woman in the wide peacock hat. Slowly, the dizziness and nausea begin to pass even if the pain doesn't, and she opens her eyes again and stares at the antique rug between her tennis shoes.

"I said *look* at me," and it takes Dancy a moment to realize that the woman's talking to her. She turns her head, and now Miss Aramat's standing much closer than before and there are two younger women standing on either side of her.

"*She* killed the Gynander?" the very tall woman on Miss Aramat's right asks skeptically. "Jesus," and she wipes her hands on the black rubber apron she's wearing, adjusts her spectacles for a better view.

The auburn-haired woman on Miss Aramat's left shakes her head, disbelieving or simply amazed. "What do you think she'd taste like, Biancabella? I have a Brazilian recipe for veal I've never tried—"

"Oh, no. We're not wasting this one in the stew pot."

"I'll have to get plantains, of course. And lots of fresh lime."

"Aramat, tell her this one's for the slab. Anyway, she looks awfully stringy."

"Yes, but I can marinate—"

"Just bring the tea, Alma," Miss Aramat says, interrupting the auburn-haired woman. "And sweets for the boy. I think there are still some blueberry tarts left from breakfast. You may call Isolde up to help you."

"But you're not really going to let Biancabella have *all* of her, are you?"

"We'll talk about it later. Get the tea. The jasmine, please."

And Alma sulks away towards the kitchen, mumbling to herself; Biancabella watches her go. "It's a wonder she's not fat as a pig," she says.

Miss Aramat kneels in front of Dancy, brushes corn-silk bangs from her white-rabbit eyes, and when Dancy tries to pull back, Dead Girl grabs a handful of her hair and holds her still.

"Does she bite?" Miss Aramat asks Dead Girl, points at the duct tape, and Dead Girl shrugs.

"She hasn't bitten me. I just got tired of listening to her talk about her goddamn angel."

"Angel?"

"She has an angel," Bobby says. "She says everyone has an angel, even me. Even Dead Girl."

"Does she really?" Miss Aramat asks the boy, most of her apprehension gone and something like delight creeping into her voice to fill the void.

"Her angel tells her where to find monsters and how to kill them."

"Angels and monsters," Miss Aramat whispers, and she smiles, her fingertips gently stroking Dancy's cheeks, skin so pale it's almost translucent. "You must be a regular Joan of Arc, then, *la pucelle de Dieu* to send us all scuttling back to Hell."

"She's a regular *nut*," Dead Girl says and draws circles in the air around her right ear.

The Bailiff laughs, and the armchair cracks again.

"Is that true, child? Are you insane?" and Miss Aramat pulls the duct tape slowly off Dancy's mouth, drops it to the carpet. It leaves behind an angry red swatch of flesh, perfect rectangle to frame her lips, and Miss Aramat leans forward and kisses her softly. Dancy stiffens, but Dead Girl's hand is there to keep her from pulling away. Only a moment, and when their mouths part, there's a faint smear of rouge left behind on Dancy's lips.

"Strange," Miss Aramat says, touching the tip of her tongue to her front teeth. "She tastes like hemlock."

"She *smells* like shit," Dead Girl sneers and yanks hard on Dancy's hair.

Miss Aramat ignores Dead Girl, doesn't take her eyes off Dancy's face.

"Do you know, child, what it meant a hundred years ago, when a man sent a woman a bouquet of hemlock? It meant, 'You will be my death.' But no, you didn't know that, did you?"

Dancy closes her eyes, remembering all the times that have been so much worse than this, all the horror and shame and sorrow to give her strength. The burning parts of her no one and nothing can ever touch, the fire where her soul used to be.

"Look at me when I talk to you," Miss Aramat says, and Dancy does, opens her eyes wide, and spits in the woman's china-doll face

"*Whore*," Dancy screams, and "*Witch*," before Dead Girl clamps a hand over her mouth.

"Guess you should've left the tape on after all," she snickers, and Miss Aramat takes a deep breath, fishes a lace handkerchief from the cuff of one sleeve, and wipes away the spittle clinging to her face. She stares silently at the damp linen for a moment while Dead Girl laughs and the Bailiff mumbles halfhearted apologies behind her.

"A needle and thread will do a better job, I think," Miss Aramat says calmly and gets up off her knees. She passes the handkerchief to Biancabella and then makes a show of smoothing the wrinkles from her dress.

Then Alma comes back with a silver serving tray, cups and saucers, cream and sugar, a teapot rimmed in gold, violets painted on the side. Porcelina's a step behind her, carrying another, smaller silver tray piled with cakes and tarts and a bowl of chocolate bonbons.

"We were out of jasmine," Alma says. "So I used the rose hip and chamomile instead."

"What's she doing up here?" and Miss Aramat points at Porcelina. "I told you to call for Isolde."

Alma frowns, sets the tray down on a walnut table near the Bailiff. "I did," she says. "But Porcelina came."

"Isolde was busy draining the corpse," Porcelina explains, and she puts her tray down beside the other. "And I've never seen vampires before."

"Is it everything you always hoped it would be?" Dead Girl purrs.

"Rose hip and chamomile sounds just wonderful," the Bailiff says, taking a saucer and two sugar cubes. "And are those poppy-seed cakes?"

Miss Aramat stares at Porcelina, who pretends not to notice, while Alma pours steaming tea into the cups.

"Yes, they are," Porcelina says. "Mary Rose baked them just this morning."

"Delightful. I haven't had a good poppy-seed cake in ages."

"Can I please have two of these?" Bobby asks, poking the sticky indigo filling of a blueberry tart lightly dusted with confectioner's sugar.

"I don't see why not, dear. They'll only go to waste otherwise."

And the sudden, swelling howl from Miss Aramat, rabid sound much too big, too wild, to ever have fit inside her body, her narrow throat, but it spills out, anyway. She turns and rushes towards the red fireplace, stretching up on tiptoes to snatch one of the swords from its bracket above the mantel. Broadsword almost as long as she is tall, but such grace in her movement, the silver arc of tempered steel, that it might weigh no more than a broomstick.

Alma shrieks and drops the violet-dappled teapot and the cup she was filling. They seem to fall forever as the sword swings round like the needle of some deadly compass, finally smashing wetly against the floor in the same instant that the blade comes to rest beneath Porcelina's chin. The razor point pressed to the soft place beneath her jawbone, only a little more pressure and she'd bleed, a thrust and the blade would slide smoothly through windpipe cartilage and into her spine.

The Bailiff stops chewing, his mouth stuffed with poppy-seed cake, the sword only inches from the end of his nose. He reaches slowly for the automatic pistol tucked into the waistband of his trousers, and Bobby turns and runs back to Dead Girl.

The grin on Miss Aramat's face is like a rictus, wide and toothy corpse grin, and "Biancabella," she says, but already the fury has drained out of her, leaving her voice barely a hoarse murmur. "Remember last winter, when you wanted to do *Salomé*? Maybe our guests would enjoy the entertainment—"

"She'll make a poor Jokanaan," Biancabella says, her eyes on the Bailiff's hand as he flips off the gun's safety and aims the barrel at Miss Aramat's head.

"Oh, *I* think she'll do just fine," and now the point of the sword draws a single scarlet bead from Porcelina's throat.

"*Please.* I'm sorry. I only wanted to see—"

" 'She is monstrous, thy daughter, she is altogether monstrous. In truth, what she has done is a *great* crime.' "

The Bailiff swallows and licks his lips, catching the last stray crumbs. "You're very thoughtful, Aramat," he says coolly, politely, as if declining another cake or another cup of jasmine tea. "Some other time, perhaps."

" 'I will not *look* at things, I will not suffer things to look at *me*—' "

"For fuck's sake," Biancabella hisses. "You know that he means it."

Aramat glances sidewise at the Bailiff and his gun, and then quickly back to Porcelina. Her grin slackens to a wistful, sour sort of smile, and she lowers the blade until the point is resting on the tea-stained carpet.

"I didn't want you thinking I wasn't a good host," she says, her eyes still fixed on Porcelina. The girl hasn't moved, stands trembling like a palsied statue; a thin trickle of blood is winding its way towards the collar of her dress.

"You understand that, Bailiff. I couldn't have you going back up to Providence and Boston, telling them all I wasn't a good host."

The Bailiff breathes out stale air and relief, and slowly he lowers his gun, easing his finger off the trigger.

"Now, you know I'd never say a thing like that, Miss Aramat." And he puts the gun away and reaches for one of the cups of tea. "I *always* look forward to our visits."

"I really wasn't expecting you until tomorrow night," she says, and Biancabella takes the sword from her hands, returns it to its place above the mantel. Miss Aramat thanks her and sits down in a salon chair near the Bailiff, but she doesn't take her eyes off Porcelina until Alma has led her from the room.

On the red sofa, Dancy turns her head and looks at Dead Girl and the frightened boy in her arms. Empty silver eyes in ageless, unaging faces. Eyes that might have seen hundreds of years or only decades, and it really makes no difference, one way or the other, when a single moment can poison a soul forever.

"Can I please have something to drink," she asks, and Dead Girl whispers in Bobby's ear. He nods his head, takes his arms from around her neck, and sits silently on the sofa next to Dancy while Dead Girl goes to get her a cup of tea.

Sometime later, though Dancy can't be sure how much later, no clocks in the red room, but an hour, surely, since they left her alone on the sofa. The contents of the leather satchel traded for a fat roll of bills, and the Bailiff turned and winked at her before he left. Miss Aramat and Biancabella followed him and Dead Girl and Bobby back out into the hall, shutting and locking the door behind them. There's only one small window, set high up on the wall past the fireplace, but if her hands weren't still strapped together with duct tape maybe she could reach it, if she stood on one of the chairs or tables.

"They'd only catch you," the black bear in the corner says. "They'd catch you and bring you right back again." She isn't very surprised that the bear's started talking to her in his gruff, sawdusty, stuffed-bear voice.

"They might not," she says. "I can run fast."

"They can run faster," the bear says, unhelpfully.

Dancy stares at the bear, at the ridiculous hat perched between his ears. She asks him if he can talk to anyone or just to her, because sometimes there are things that can only talk to her, things only she can hear because no one else will ever listen.

"I talked to the man who shot me," the bear growls. "And I spoke to Candida once, but she told me she'd throw me out with the trash if I ever did it again."

"What will they do to me?" Dancy asks, and when the bear doesn't answer her, she asks again. "What are they going to do to me, bear?"

"I'd rather not say."

"Stupid bear. You probably don't have any idea what goes on in this house."

The bear grumbles to itself and stares straight ahead with its glass eyeballs. "I wish I didn't," he says. "I wish the taxidermist had forgotten to give me eyes to see or ears to hear. I wish the hunter had left me to rot in the woods."

"They're very wicked women," Dancy says, watching the door now instead of the bear. He doesn't reply, tired of listening to her or maybe he's gone back to sleep, whatever it is dead bears do instead of sleep. She gets up and crosses the room, stands in front of two paintings hung side by side above a potted plant. Both are portraits of the bodies of dead women.

"Is this a riddle?" she asks the bear.

"I don't answer riddles," the bear replies.

"That's not what I asked you."

"If I still had a stomach," the bear says, "I'd like one of those chocolate bonbons there," and then he doesn't point at the silver serving platter because he can't move, and Dancy decides she's better off ignoring him and looks at the two paintings, instead.

The one on the right shows a naked corpse so emaciated that Dancy can make out the sharp jut of its hipbones, the peaks and valleys of its ribs. Sunken, hollow eyes, gaping mouth, and the woman's left breast has sagged so far that it's settled in her armpit. She lies on a bare slab, and there's only a hard wooden block to prop up her skull.

"You could put one into my mouth. I might remember how to taste it."

"Shut up, bear," and now Dancy examines the painting on her left. This dead woman might only be sleeping, if not for the grief on the face of the old man seated there at her side. Her hands folded neatly across her breasts, and she's dressed in a satin gown and lies on a bed covered with white roses, two soft pillows tucked beneath her head.

"It *is* a riddle," Dancy says. "One is the truth, and one isn't. Or they're both true, but only partly true. They're both lies, without the other."

"Give me a bonbon, and I'll tell you which," the stuffed bear growls.

"You don't answer riddles. You said so."

"I'll make an exception."

"I don't think you even know."

"I'm dead. Dead bears know lots of things," and Dancy's thinking about that, trying to decide whether or not she could even get a piece of the candy all the way up into the bear's mouth with her wrists tied together.

"All right," she says, but then there's a rustling sound behind her, like dry, October leaves in a cold breeze, and the air smells suddenly of cinnamon and ice.

I never knew ice had a smell, she thinks, turning, and there's a very pretty boy standing on the other side of the room, watching her. The door's still closed, or he shut it again. He's tall and very slender, maybe a little older than she is, and wearing a black velvet dress with a dark green symbol like an hourglass embroidered over his flat chest. His long hair is the exact same green as the hourglass, and his eyes are the color of starlight.

"Hello, Dancy," he says, and takes a step towards her. He's barefoot and has a silver ring on each of his toes. "Who were you talking to?"

"The bear," she says, and the boy smiles and reaches into a pocket of his dress; he takes out a small stoppered bottle and holds it up where she can see. The glass is the amber color of pine sap or deep swamp pools stained by rotting vegetation.

"The Ladies have asked me to speak to you," he tells her. "I've brought them something quite precious, but they thought you should see it first. And, I admit, I've been wanting to see you for myself. You have a lot of people talking, Dancy Flammarion."

"Did you know he was coming?" she asks the bear, or her angel, it doesn't really matter which, since neither of them answers her.

"You're not exactly what any of us expected. Why did you come to Savannah? Who did you come here to kill?"

"I'm not sure," she says, and that much is true, all her dreams after Waycross, all the things she sees in dark hours, only bits and tattered pieces, something broken and there wasn't time to figure out how all the parts fit together.

"You didn't come for the Ladies?"

"They're not real monsters," she says. "They're nothing but witches and perverts and cannibals. They're all crazy, but they're not real monsters at all."

"No," he says. "They're not. Did you come for me, then? Did you come for my master or one of the Parsifal?"

"I don't know."

"Did you come for this?" and the boy in the black dress holds the bottle out to her, and Dancy looks back at the bear again, imagines a story where he springs suddenly to life and leaps across the room to devour this strange boy in a single bite.

"No. I don't even know what that is," she says.

For a moment, the boy doesn't say anything else, watches her with his brilliant star-shine eyes, eyes to read her mind, her soul, to ferret out lies and half-truths. They're starting to make her feel lightheaded, those eyes, and she glances down at the floor.

"Do I frighten you, Dancy?"

"No," she lies. "I'm not scared of you."

"Look at me then," he says, and when she does, Dancy sees that she isn't standing by the bear and the dead-woman paintings anymore, but sitting on the red sofa again, and the duct tape binding her hands is gone. The pretty boy is sitting beside her, on her left, staring down at the amber bottle in his hand. The glass looks very old, oily, prismatic. He shakes it, and inside something buzzes and flickers to life, lightning-bug flicker, and soon the bottle has begun to glow as brightly as the fancy lamps set around the room, and she can't look directly at it anymore.

"Some people still think that it's the Grail," he says. "It isn't, of course. The alchemist Petrus Bonus thought it might be a splinter of the *lapis exilis*, but it isn't that, either. For a long time, it was lost. It turned up a few years ago in a Portuguese fisherman's nets, trapped inside this bottle. The fisherman died trying to open it."

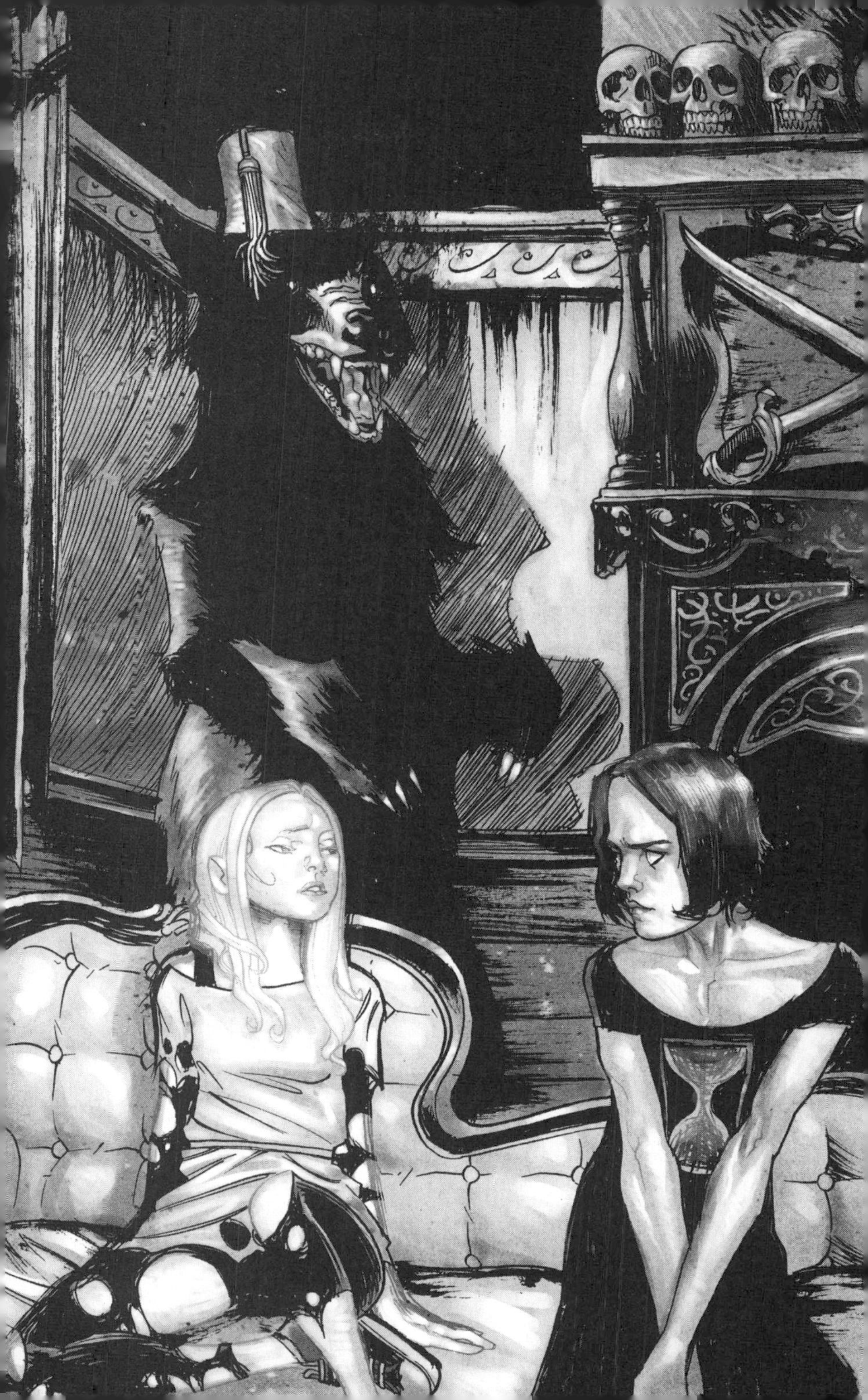

"So what is it?" Dancy asks, trying not to hear the low, thrumming voices woven into the light from the bottle. A rumbling thunderstorm choir to rattle her teeth, to make ashes of her bones and soot of her white flesh.

"Just a toy. An unfinished experiment. Some forgotten, second-rate wizard's silly trinket."

"Then it isn't precious at all," Dancy says, and her eyes have started to hurt so badly that she looks away. Tears are streaming down her cheeks, and the thrumming sound is starting to make her head ache.

"It's quite useless, but there are people who would die for it. There are people who would *kill* for it."

"You're just another riddle, aren't you?" Dancy whispers. "I'm sick of riddles." She's holding her fingertips to her temples, eyes squeezed shut, the voices stuck inside her head now and trying to force their way out through her skull.

"But that's all there is, I'm afraid. In the whole, wide, irredeemable world, that's all there is, finally."

"No. That's not true," Dancy says. "There's pain—"

"But why? *Why* is there pain, Dancy?"

"So there can be an end to pain," and she wishes on the names of all the saints and angels she can remember that the boy will stop talking, stop asking her questions, kill her and get it over with. She doesn't want to be alive when the voices from the bottle find their way out of her head.

"What do you hear, Dancy Flammarion? The voices, what do they sing for you? What songs do they sing for martyrs and monster slayers?"

"They *hate* you," she says and then bites down hard on the end of her tongue so that she won't say anything else, nothing else she isn't supposed to say. Her mouth tastes like salt and wheat pennies and rainwater.

"That's nothing I didn't already know. What do they sing for my oblation, for your sacrifice?"

The throb behind her eyes folding and unfolding, becoming something unbearable, unthinkable, that stretches itself across the sizzling sky, running on forever or so far it may as well be forever. A choir of agony, razor-shard crescendo, and "Haven't you ever tried to open the bottle?" Dancy asks the boy, because she can't keep it all inside herself any longer.

And for her answer, the rustling, autumn sound again, though this time she thinks it's actually more like wings, leathery bat wings or the nervous wings of small birds, the flutter of ten thousand flapping wings, and Dancy knows that if she opens her eyes it won't be the boy sitting next to her. Something else entirely, something much closer to whatever he really is, and now the red room stinks of roadkill and shit and garbage left to slowly rot beneath the summer sun.

"It's only a toy," she says.

"That's what he's afraid of," the stuffed bear growls from across the room, and Dancy laughs, because she knows he's telling the truth. Dead bears don't like riddles, either, and when she tries to stand up she falls, tumbles like a dropped teapot that would never stop falling if she had a choice, would never have to shatter like the china-doll woman who shattered a long, long time ago and the Savannah River washed most of the pieces away to the sea.

Dancy opens her eyes, and the bottle's lying on the floor in front of her. The roaring, hurtful voices inside drip from her nostrils and lips and ears, a sticky molasses-dark puddle on the rug, and "Pick it up," the thing that isn't a boy in a dress snarls, making words from the tumult of feathers and hurricane wind. "You're dying, anyway. There's nothing it can do to you. Show me the trick."

"There *isn't* any trick," she says, reaching for the bottle. "It's only a toy."

"No," the bear growls. "Don't you touch it. Make him do his own dirty work," but she's already holding the bottle, so light in her hand, so warm, a balm to soothe the pain eating her alive, and she looks up into the maelstrom spinning in the bruised place hung a few feet above the red sofa. The counterclockwise gyre of snapping, twig-thin bones and mockingbird quills, the eyes like swollen, seeping wounds, and *here*, this part she remembers, this moment from a nightmare of hungry, whirling fire and dying birds.

"You should have tried the window," the bear says, and Dancy vomits, nothing much in her stomach but the tea that Dead Girl let her drink, but she vomits, anyway.

"It *knows* you, Dancy Flammarion. Before you were born, it knew you. Before the sun sparked to life, it was already calling you here."

"I don't want it," she coughs and wipes her mouth.

"*You* know *the trick. We* know *you know the trick*," and the thing in the air above the sofa is screaming, screeching, turning faster and faster, and bits of itself are coming loose and drifting slowly down to the floor. Wherever they land, the rug scorches and smolders.

"*Open it!*"

Dancy sits up, and for a moment she stares deep into the wheel, the paradox-still point at its absolute center—consuming and blossoming heart, nothing and everything there all at once. "Abracadabra," she whispers, her throat gone raw and her head coming apart at the seams, and she throws the bottle as hard as she can. It arcs end over end, and the pretty boy with star-shine eyes (and she sees that he *has* become a boy again, that the boy was there somewhere, all along) is scrambling after it. When the bottle hits the wall, it bursts into a spray of powdered glass and blue-golden flame that rises quickly towards the ceiling. A sparkling ruin that twines itself into a hammer, a wave, a fist of the purest light, and as the pain leaves her head and the world slips kindly away to leave her alone in darkness, the hammer falls, and the only sounds left are the promises that monsters make before they die.

"Is it over?" Mary Rose asks, speaking very quietly, and Biancabella holds an index finger up to her lips, hush.

The Ladies of the Stephens Ward Tea League and Society of Resurrectionists wait together in the long hall outside the door to the Crimson Room. Miss Aramat is sitting on the stairs, alone with Porcelina's body in her arms, singing softly to herself or to Porcelina's ghost—*Blacks and bays, dapples and grays, when you wake you shall have all the pretty little horses.* The bread knife she used to cut Porcelina's throat lies at her feet, sticky with drying blood. The house on East Hall Street is quiet now, breathless in the battered silence after the storm, and there's only Miss Aramat's voice and the obstinate ticking of the grandfather clock by the stairs, the distant ticking of other clocks in other rooms.

All the things they've heard, or only think they've heard, since the Bailiff left and Samuel's boy went into the room with his bottle and the albino girl, the inescapable, inevitable moment of Porcelina's death, but all of it not half so terrible as this silence. This waiting, and once Candida put her hand on the doorknob and pulled it quickly back again, her palm scalded raw by the cold.

"He used us," Isolde murmurs. "He *lied* to us."

"They *both* used us," Emily replies, then the look from Miss Aramat enough that neither of them says anything more.

Just the clocks and pretty little horses and the long, last hour before dawn.

And then the knob turns, finally, the tumblers of the lock rolling themselves, the irrelevant key in Biancabella's pocket, and the door swings open. Dancy Flammarion stands silhouetted in lamplight and a weirder, flaxen glow, fairy fire, foxfire, that seems to shine from somewhere just behind her. A power in that light, and dignity, and darker things that will haunt the dreams of the Ladies for the rest of their lives. But the glow fades immediately away when she steps out into the shadow-strewn hallway, and she's only the Bailiff's hitchhiker again.

Dancy holds one of the swords from over the fireplace gripped tightly in both hands. Her face is streaked with tears and blood and vomit, and Biancabella notices that one of her shoes is untied.

Miss Aramat stops singing. "What did you do to him?" she asks. "Is he dead? Did you kill him?"

"He would have let you open the bottle for him," Dancy says. "He would have let you all die trying."

Miss Aramat looks down at Porcelina's head in her lap, and she smiles sadly and strokes the dead girl's matted hair.

"What was in it?" she whispers.

"Nothing meant for you. Nothing meant for him, either."

"I tried to tell her," Miss Aramat says, wiping a bloody smear from underneath Porcelina's left eye. "I tried to tell her we wanted nothing to do with the goddamned thing."

"Is that why you killed her?" Dancy asks her.

Miss Aramat wipes away another splotch of blood, and then she closes Porcelina's eyes. "I can't remember why I killed her," she says. "I knew for certain, only a moment ago, but now I can't remember. Do you know, Biancabella?"

"You were angry," Biancabella replies, keeping her eyes on the sword in Dancy's hands. "You were afraid."

"Was I? Well, there you go, then. Biancabella's hardly ever wrong."

"Are you going to kill us all now?" Alma asks Dancy. "We wouldn't really have hurt you, you know, not really. We were only—"

"Jesus *Christ*," Biancabella hisses. "You only wanted to cook her with plantains. Shut up, or I'll kill you myself."

"I'm leaving now," Dancy says, and she takes another step away from the door to the Crimson Room, still holding the sword out in front of her like a shield. Alma and Candida step out of her way, and "Thank you, oh, thank you," Alma gushes. "We wouldn't have hurt you, not really. We would never, ever—"

"Alma, I *told* you to shut the fuck up!"

"I'm sorry," and then Alma's backing away from Dancy and Biancabella both, presses herself insect flat against the wall. "I won't say anything else, I promise. I'm sorry I ever said anything at all."

"Get the hell out of here, girl," Biancabella growls. "*Now*, before I change my mind. I don't give a shit what happened in there; you couldn't kill all of us."

Dancy glances at the sword and then nods once, because she knows that Biancabella's probably right, and what she came to do is finished, so it doesn't matter anyway. She turns and hurries towards the front door. Outside, the first watery hints of dawn, gray-blue wash through the window set into the front door, and she never thought she'd see daylight again.

"Stop!" Miss Aramat shouts, and when she stands up, Porcelina's body rolls forward and tumbles loudly to the bottom of the stairs.

So close, Dancy thinks, *so close*, only two or three more steps and she would have been out the door and running down the street, and she wouldn't have looked back even once.

"It doesn't end this way," Miss Aramat says, and when Dancy turns around, the china-doll woman's holding a revolver pointed at her. "Not in my house, missy. You don't come into my house and make threats and then walk out the front door like nothing's happened."

"Let her go," Biancabella says. "It's not worth it."

"We have to have a feast to remember Porcelina by, don't we? We'll have to have something *special*," and Miss Aramat pulls the trigger. There's a small, hard *click* as the hammer falls on an empty chamber.

"I didn't come for you," Dancy says, and she tightens her grip on the sword because it's the only thing left to hold onto. "You're nothing but a wicked, crazy woman."

"And *you*, you think you're any better? You're so goddamn high and mighty, standing there on the side of the goddamn angels, and we're nothing but shit, is that it?"

"Please, Aramat," Biancabella begs. "We'll find something else for Porcelina's feast, something truly special. We'll take the car and drive down to St. Augustine—"

"*Look* at her, Biancabella. *She's* the monster. She has the marks," and Miss Aramat pulls the revolver's trigger again, and again there's only the impotent taunt of the hammer falling on an empty chamber.

"Let her go, Aramat," and now Biancabella's moving towards the stairs. She shoves Isolde aside and almost trips over Porcelina's corpse. "She's *nothing* to us. She's just someone's fucking puppet."

"I didn't come for you," Dancy says again.

" 'I *will* kiss thy mouth, Jokanaan,' " Miss Aramat whispers, and the third time she squeezes the trigger the revolver explodes in a deafening flash of fire and thunder, tearing itself apart, and the shrapnel takes her hands and face with it, buries a chunk of steel the size of a grape between her eyes. One of the fragments grazes Biancabella's left cheek, digging a bloody furrow from the corner of her mouth to her ear, and she stands, helpless, at the bottom of the stairs as Aramat crumples and falls.

And Dancy Flammarion doesn't wait to see whatever does or doesn't come next. She drops the sword and runs, out the front door of the big house on East Hall Street, across the wide yard, and the new day wraps her safe in redeeming charcoal wings and hides her steps.

Not yet noon and already a hundred degrees in the shade, and the Bailiff is sitting alone on the rusted rear bumper of the

Monte Carlo drinking a Coke. The sun a proper demon overhead, and he holds the cool bottle pressed to his forehead for a
moment and squints into the mirage shimmer writhing off the
blacktop. Dancy Flammarion is walking towards him up the
entrance ramp to the interstate, a small girl shape beneath a huge
black umbrella, coming slowly, stubbornly through the heat-
bent summer day. A semi rushes past, roars past, and there's
wind for a moment, though it isn't a cool wind. The truck rattles
away, and once again the only sound is the droning rise and fall
of cicadas. The Bailiff finishes his Coke and tosses the empty
bottle into the marsh at the side of the road; he takes a blue
paisley bandanna from his back pocket and wipes the sweat from
his face and bald head.

"A man needs a hat in a place like this," he says, and Dancy
stops a few feet from the car and watches him. She's wearing a
pair of sunglasses that look like she must have found them lying
by the side of the road, the left lens cracked and the bridge held
together with a knotted bit of nylon fishing twine.

"You set me up, old man," she says to him. "You set us all up,
didn't you?"

"Maybe a nice straw Panama hat, something to keep the sun
from cooking his brains. Didn't Clark Gable wear one of those
in *Gone with the Wind*?"

"Was it the bottle, or the boy?"

The Bailiff stuffs the blue bandanna back into his trouser
pocket and winks at Dancy. "It was the bottle," he says. "And
the boy, and some other people you best hope you never have to
meet face to face."

"And the women?"

"No. It didn't really ever have anything much to do with the
Ladies."

"Aramat's dead," she says, and then another truck roars by,
whipping the trash and grit at the side of the interstate into a

whirlwind. When it's gone, Dancy wipes the dust off her clothes, and "It was an accident," she says.

"Well now, that's a shame, I guess. I'd honestly hoped it wouldn't come to that," and the Bailiff shades his eyes and glances up at the sun. "But it was always only a matter of time. Some people are just too damn mean and crazy for their own good. Anyway, I imagine Biancabella can take care of things now."

"I don't understand."

"What don't you understand, Dancy Flammarion?"

"The boy. I mean, whose side are you on?"

And the Bailiff laughs softly to himself, then, and reaches for the bandanna again.

"You've got a lot to learn, child. You're a goddamn holy terror, all right, but you've got a *lot* to learn."

She stares at him silently, her eyes hidden behind the broken sunglasses, while the Bailiff blows his nose and the cicadas scream at each other.

"Can I have my duffel bag back," she says. "I left it in your car."

"Wouldn't you rather have a ride? This sun isn't good for regular folks. I hate to think what it'll do to an albino. You're starting to turn pink already."

Dancy looks at her forearm, frowns, and then looks back at the Bailiff.

"What about the others?" she asks.

The Bailiff raps his knuckles twice on the trunk. "Dead to the world," he says. "At least until sunset. And I owe you one after—"

"You don't owe me nothing," Dancy says.

"Then think of it as a temporary cease-fire. It'll be a nice change, having someone to talk to who still breathes."

Dancy stares at the Monte Carlo, at the Bailiff, and then at the endless, broiling ribbon of I-16 stretching away north and west towards Atlanta and the mountains.

"But I'm not even sure where I'm going."

"I thought that's why you have angels, to tell you these things?"

"They will, eventually."

"Well, it's only a couple of hours to Macon. How's that for a start?"

In the marsh, a bird calls out, long-legged swamp bird, and Dancy turns her head and watches as the egret spreads its wide alabaster wings and flaps away across the cordgrass, something black and squirming clutched in its long beak.

"It's a start," she says, but waits until the egret is only a smudge against the blue-white sky before she closes the umbrella and follows the Bailiff into the shade of the car.

For Dame Darcy

The Well of Stars and Shadow

Through the deepening slash-pine shadows, the dim and fading shafts of twilight falling pale through the high branches of Shrove Wood, and Dancy Flammarion follows the familiar twists and turns of Wampee Creek. The cinnamon ferns and saw palmetto grown waist high to an eight-year-old, understory carpet of rust fronds and emerald-sharp leaves, and she watches the uneven ground, mindful where she puts her feet, watching for snakes and steel-jawed traps laid among the pine straw. Traps set for raccoon and bobcats, but they're just as happy to snap shut on little-girl ankles, even this strange albino child who can only go out to play when the sun turns fat and red and sinks slow into the swamp.

"You watch yourself now. Don't go getting lost or hurt," her mother or her grandmother always says, and "I won't. I'm very, very careful," Dancy always reassures them. "I know my way," and she does, the long mile and a half between their cabin and the place where Wampee Creek spills out into the wide, peat-dark lake that no one has ever bothered to name. But they worry for her anyway, this girl all they have left in the world, and sometimes, hazy gray evenings when the cicadas are a little quieter than they should be or her mother doesn't like the look of the stars rising over the trees, Dancy carries her grandmother's crucifix in the bib pocket of her overalls, near her heart, and maybe a sprig of pennyroyal or dried angelica root wrapped in a white cotton handkerchief, as well.

"Never hurt nobody yet to be too cautious," her grandmother might say, and "Better safe than sorry," her mother might nod. So Dancy carries their charms, and wears her own tarnished St. Christopher's medal, and watches where she puts her feet.

A sudden splash, and she stops, focuses her pink eyes on the crystal waters gurgling between low yellow-white limestone banks. *Just an ol' bullfrog*, she thinks, scared off by the sound of her boots, the dry crunch of pine needles underfoot, the brittle snap of twigs. "I ain't after you today, Mr. Frog," she says, her voice big in the still and the half-light of the wood. "If I was, you never woulda heard me coming."

Wampee Creek whispers back to her in its secret, frog-hiding language, conspiracy of moss and ripples, and Dancy Flammarion shrugs her bony shoulders and looks up at the sky. Only indigo scraps and patches visible between the boughs, but enough that she can see it'll be dark soon, and she'd rather make it all the way to Mr. Jube's shack before the greedy shadows swell and swallow everything, the world tumbling down the night's velvet throat, leaving her to pick her way blindly through the trees. Then it won't matter how hard she squints and stares at the ground, then the snakes and traps and stump holes will have her at their mercy, and she learned a long time ago that mercy isn't one of the virtues of night in the wood.

"See you sometime else, frog," she says and starts walking again, and by the time Dancy comes to the lake there's only the slimmest rind of dusk hanging low in the sky and an icy, white sliver of moon is rising above the pines and cypress crowded like thirsty giants around the shore.

Rain and rust and the baking north Florida sun, time and all its corrosions, to leave only rotting bits of ironmongery where once there was a town; a hundred years ago, and the Hebbard Lumber Company of Philadelphia sliced a path through the canebrake wilderness and stitched it up again with steel rails and creosote crossties. The men who came to cut the trees, to turn pine and sycamore and bay into weekly wages and callused hands, a billion board feet of timber hauled from the swamp by the company's clattering, steam-breath engines, and maybe no one ever gave the lake a name but the town that grew up around it was christened Hebbard's Mill. 1904, and the company built shotgun houses and a general store, raised a church and school for the children of the men, ran telephone lines all the way from Milligan, and for two decades this was somewhere.

And then, suddenly, it simply wasn't anymore.

A cholera epidemic in '21 and rumors of scandal back in Philadelphia, embezzlement and doctored books, death, and, finally, nervous whispers about the lake, blue lights seen floating above the black waters late at night. Blue lights or lights the color of infection, gangrene will-o'-the-wisps, and the men began to leave a year before the company took the town apart, pulled nails from weathered slats, shipped away the pieces that could be sold or used elsewhere and left the rest to decay, a belated offering to the swamp so at least maybe the bad luck wouldn't follow them.

Nothing remaining now but the scattered hulks of steel— boilers and steam pipes lost amongst the tall brown grass and dead leaves, abandoned washtubs and the disintegrating skeletons of company trucks; Hebbard's Mill gone all the way back to the forgotten gods of the Apalachee, back to the bears and alligators, and hardly ever anyone out here but Mr. Jube in his shack to tend the small cemetery set back among the live oaks and magnolias.

Dancy Flammarion pauses where the clear, clean waters of Wampee Creek bleed themselves away into the peat-stained lake, always a moment's hesitation because there are ghosts here, ghosts and worse things than ghosts, she thinks; but then she sees the lantern burning bright on Mr. Jube's porch, the warm and welcoming orange-white glow of burning kerosene, and the old man waves to her from his rocking chair. She looks over her shoulder at the forest, the inky spaces between the trees, the trail leading back the way she's come, back to her mother and grandmother and their small cabin near Eleanore Road. They've never met Mr. Jube, but sometimes they send him a jar of blackberry preserves or a loaf of bread, anyway, trusting Dancy, that she's wise enough to know good men from bad.

She walks quickly along the muddy cattail-choked shore, the short path he keeps clear for her, and in another moment, she's standing safe on the porch. Mr. Jube smiles his wide, false-toothed smile for her, tobacco-yellowed dentures and his skin the color of molasses, a full white beard to make up for his bald head. "Well now," he says, "what you doin' all the way out here this evening, Miss Dancy?"

"I never had to have a reason before," she says, and "No," he replies. "I guess you never did. Just, some nights, well, some nights ain't the same as all the others."

"Want me to go back home again?" and the old man stares at her and rubs his beard a moment.

"No, girl. Now that you're here, you'd best stay a while. What's wrong with your arm there?"

"Nothing. I got scratched up by some creeper briars, that's all," she says and shows him the pricked and bleeding place on her left forearm, the small red welts on her pale skin.

"Well, we ought to put something on that, some iodine, don't you think?" and before she can say yes or no, he gets up. "You just wait right here," he tells her, points to the crooked stool near his rocker, one leg longer than the other two, or two legs shorter than the third, and she obediently sits down for him. The screen door slams loud, echoes far across the lake, and Dancy waits alone until Mr. Jube comes back with a small bottle of iodine and a cotton ball.

"It don't hurt much," she says, trying not to wince, pretending the antiseptic doesn't sting as he dabs the brownish liquid on her outstretched arm. "It's just a scratch."

"Never can tell with briars. Better safe than sorry."

"You sound like my momma," Dancy says and frowns.

"Is that a fact?"

"She says that all the time."

"Well, then, your momma must be a right smart lady," and when he's done, Mr. Jube screws the cap back on the bottle and blows on Dancy's arm a moment, his breath like stale pipe smoke and apple cider. Then he tosses the cotton ball away into the hungry darkness waiting at the edges of the porch and sits in his chair again; the wood creaks and pops, and he looks at the label on the bottle before setting it down near his feet.

"She taught me how to read," Dancy tells him. "I've read all her books. I've read the whole Bible."

But Dancy's already told him that a dozen other times, and Mr. Jube only nods his bald head for her and stares out at the night and the wide, still pool. His eyes almost the same color as the water, old man eyes grown suddenly distant and alert, and she knows he's listening to the lake.

"Did you hear something?" she asks, but he doesn't reply, leans forward a few inches and stares intently into the dark. So Dancy sits quietly and watches the restless cloud of bugs flitting about the lantern's chimney, waiting patiently until he's ready to talk to her again.

"How 'bout a game of checkers?" he asks, finally, sitting up straight in his rocking chair. "Think you're up to a few games a checkers tonight?"

"Sure," she says, even though she really doesn't like checkers and doesn't want to play, would much rather he told her stories about his days in New Orleans and St. Louis, or showed her the snakes and frogs and turtles that he catches to sell to the men from Tallahassee.

"I'll make us a pot of coffee," he says, still watching the night. "I got some jellybeans, too. I've been saving out all the red ones for you."

"I like the green ones best."

Mr. Jube shakes his head, sighs, and looks away from the lake. "Damn. I coulda swore it was the red ones you liked best."

"I like the red ones, too." And she sits on the stool while he glances back towards the water one more time. That look on his face that she's never sure means he's afraid or he's curious, both maybe, and after a few moments more he stands up and takes the lantern off its hook, and Dancy Flammarion follows him inside.

Dancy not talking because she knows that Mr. Jube doesn't like to talk or have to listen to anyone else talk while he's playing checkers, not even when he's letting her win. She sucks on a yellow jellybean, letting the tart and sugary coating slowly dissolve in her mouth, stripping the candy down to its gummy, bland center, and Mr. Jube taps his fingers lightly on the edge of the table, *tap, tap, tap, tap*, deliberate woodpecker noise to make her wonder what he's thinking about. His face all wrinkled concentration and his eyes fixed on the board between them, but she knows his mind is somewhere else; he takes a sip of his black coffee and slides a red checker towards her. Dancy jumps it, and two more besides, and Mr. Jube scratches his head and pretends to be surprised.

"Now why didn't I see that?" he says.

" 'Cause you ain't trying, that's why," Dancy says and spits what's left of the yellow jellybean out into the palm of her left hand.

"Yeah? Well, maybe, or maybe you're just gettin' too good for me."

Dancy adds the three captured checkers to the neat stack in front of her. "King me," she says and pops the jellybean back into her mouth.

"Look at that. Now you're gettin' my checkers all sticky."

"It isn't any fun when you don't even try to win. I don't want to play anymore. Tell me a story, instead."

"Bad luck to leave a game unfinished."

Dancy stares at him for a moment, trying to remember if she's ever heard it was bad luck not to finish a game of checkers, the sort of thing her grandmother would have taught her, if it was true, so she's pretty sure he's just making it up.

"I ain't never heard—"

"You *haven't* ever heard."

"I *haven't* ever heard it was bad luck not to finish a game of checkers."

"Lots of things you ain't heard, child."

Dancy fishes another jellybean from the big bag on the table, a pink one, and she thinks about putting it back because the pink ones taste like Pepto-Bismol.

"That's why I come way out here to talk to you," she says and puts the pink jellybean back in the bag, takes out an orange one, instead.

"I look like a schoolteacher?"

"I ain't never seen a schoolteacher," Dancy mumbles around the orange jellybean, "so I wouldn't know if you do or not."

"Bet your momma don't let you sass her like that," Mr. Jube says and looks over his shoulder at the door, at the dark windows on either side of it like bookends.

"You could tell me again about the time you saw the *loup-garou*, or the time you caught the two-headed snapping turtle and—"

"I never said that was a snapper. Just an old cooter terrapin, that's all," Mr. Jube says, still looking at the door, and Dancy sighs and swallows the orange jellybean without bothering to chew it.

"Or the time you went deep-sea fishin' and—"

"*Hush* a minute, girl," the old man growls at her, holds up one index finger like he's pointing the way to Heaven, so Dancy sits still and waits for him to be finished with whatever's gotten his attention. Whatever he's listening to, listening for, and then she hears it, too, and "Oh," she whispers. "What *is* that, Mr. Jube?"

"You just sit right there, Dancy," he whispers back, "and don't you say nothin' else, not one word, till I say so," and now she's afraid, the urgent tremble in his voice and this sound she's never heard before; something far away, but coming closer, rumble so deep she feels it in her bones, her teeth, all the way down in her soul.

"You shouldn'ta come out here tonight, Dancy," Mr. Jube says. "But you didn't know."

Dancy shakes her head, *no, no, no,* she couldn't have known, and she grips the edge of the table, grits her teeth together tight and the rumbling sound rises and falls like hurricane breath and locomotive wrecks. The earth splitting apart beneath her feet, and the sky above her head broken by the weight of the stars; the bag of jellybeans falls over, spilling a rainbow spray on the cabin floor, and the checkers skitter and dance across the board.

"I shoulda told you all this a long time ago," he says. "Guess I shoulda told you a hell of a lot of things . . ." but she can hardly hear him now, regretful words buried deep in the roar, and across the room a quart Ball mason jar full of pennies and nickels tumbles off a windowsill and bursts. Dancy shuts her eyes tight, not wanting to see what could ever make such a terrible racket. So loud there's no room left for anything else, the whole wide world pressed flat and dry and silent as an old briar rose held forever between Bible-thin pages, the world pressed brittle, and she can't even remember how to pray.

The salty, copper taste of blood, sharp pain nailed between her eyes, and "You make it stop!" she screams. "Oh God, Mr. Jube, make it stop right *now!*" and it does, meanest splinter of the empty moment between her frantic heartbeats, space between the throbbing in her head, and the only thing left behind is the murmuring swamp outside the cabin—the frogs and cricket fiddles, cicadas and night birds. Dancy slowly opens her eyes, blinks at the back of Mr. Jube's bald head, and when she wipes her mouth on the back of her hand, there's a smear of spit and crimson.

I bit my tongue, she thinks. *That's all. I just bit my own stupid tongue.*

"Now, you do what I said," Mr. Jube tells her, firm and a bright hint of fear around the edges of his voice, the way her grandmother sounded the day that Dancy found a rabid fox hiding under their back porch.

"This is all gonna be done and finished 'fore you even know it. You listenin' to me, child?"

"Jesus, ain't it done *already?*" she asks, and he glares over his shoulder at her.

"What d'you think your momma would think about you blasphemin' like that?"

"I bet you she'd say something worse'n that, if she was here."

Mr. Jube shakes his head and turns back to the door, the blank, unseeing windows. "Well, she *ain't* here, so you're gonna mind me. And this *ain't* done just yet. We got a little bit more to come. But we gonna be fine, Dancy. You do exactly what I say and everything's gonna be jake."

"Yes, sir," she says, trying hard not to let him hear how scared she really is, trying to feel the way a grownup would feel, brave like her grandmother when she shot the rabid fox.

"What you want me to do?"

"Stay where you are, and I want you to start counting backwards from one hundred. Not out loud, just start counting to yourself, in your head."

"Backwards from a hundred."

"And don't you say a word, girl, no matter what you see. Think about them numbers. Imagine you got a stick and you're drawing numbers in the sand. When you get done drawing one, imagine that you take your left foot and wipe the sand smooth again before you draw the next number. Can you do that?"

"Yes, sir. I can do that."

"Then we both gonna be right as rain," he tells her, and a second later there's a knock at the door. Dancy looks at the checkerboard, bad luck not to finish a game, and wishes she'd stayed home and watched her mother sew, wishes that she'd followed Eleanore Road out to the hilly place where she sits sometimes and gazes across the tops of the pines at the faraway lights of Milligan, wishes she were any place instead of in this cabin at the edge of the black lake at the end of Wampee Creek.

"Now, Dancy," Mr. Jube says. "You start countin' now," and she does.

Moonlight and magnolia, starlight in your hair, all the world a dream, a dream come true, did it really happen, was I really there, was I really there with you . . .

A vast lion of white connect-the-dots fire, frigid pinpricks against eternity, and the imaginary lions men draw between the stars. Capricious swipe of a twinkling paw, and light falls from midnight autumn skies, November 1833, and the glowing dust of comets and all the things a small blue world brushes against in its lonely race around the sun; bright and frozen things to burn as they streak and scream and fall, falling since the universe drew its first scalding breath and coughed up Creation, but finally falling down. Angels down from Heaven, and fingers groping in a dark place touch something soft and cold that burns—

We lived our little drama, we kissed in a field of white.

November 13, 1833, and the wide southern night sky gone bright as noon. Startled men and women coming suddenly awake in their beds, squinting, dazzled eyes for the darkness that wasn't there. And *This must be judgment day*, they whispered and listened for Gabriel's trumpets and seraphim explanation. Terrified, amazed, humbled at this end, surely, this ice-white curtain of flame drawing closed across history, and there are times when all men pray to one thing or another.

I can't forget the glamour, your eyes held a tender light, and stars fell . . .

Inevitable intersections, convergences, the crossing of ancient, invisible paths: 1799, 1833, 1866, 1867, 1966, forever and ever, and the lion swats at glittering baubles hung for its or no one else's pleasure.

. . . and stars fell . . .

Mobile Commercial Register (Nov. 13, 1833)—Last night, or rather very early this morning, the vault of Heaven presented a brilliant spectacle, differing from any we have ever heard of. We regret that our slumbers were so heavy as to prevent our observing it, but a great number of our acquaintance were roused by their servants, to whom it had imparted no small degree of alarm. Meteors of the description commonly termed *falling stars*, but of unusual splendor and magnitude, were seen shooting in every part of the heavens, in every line of direction below horizontal. Some from above appeared descending, but as is usual in the same phenomenon as it ordinarily appears in single instances, they were generally extinguished before coming in range with the level of the earth. Hundreds were seen darting at the same moment. Their vivid coruscations continued for hours, and only ceased when the light of day compelled them to hide their diminishing heads, so that for any thing we know to the contrary, they may still be disporting in the upper air.

Philosophers have not been able to offer any plausible theory in explanation of the description of meteors. To say that they are electric, or that they proceed from the spontaneous combustion of inflammable vapor, is only to evade rational enquiry by the employment of learned words. Before either of these principles can be admitted as sufficient causes, it must be shewn in what manner electricity can be accumulated in an atmosphere pure and dry, or what there is in such a region of the air as to develope explosive gas, or to ignite it after it has been produced. We believe it is admitted that no branch of scientific investigation so completely puts the ingenuity of philosophy at defence, as meteorology.

And some smoldering something flashes swift across Mississippi and Alabama and marsh-gray Florida skies, one more momentary inferno in a burning dawn, the blink of a million frightened eyes, and it plunges sizzling and sputtering into a deep black pool. A splash and charcoal wisp of steam, and the waters take it down into the soothing, fish-secret silt, the slime and a blackness not so perfect as that former, lost Paradise, but the pain that seared away its soul is cooled, and in a hundred years it will hardly remember the lion's paw, the flames, the fall, the innocent eons of weightless vacuum before gravity's deceiving pull.

I never planned, in my imagination, a situation so heavenly, a fairy land where no one else could enter, and in the center, just you and me, dear . . .

November 13, 1833, and for seventy years nothing and no one looked into the pool but soulless alligator eyes and wildcats and the Indians who were afraid to stare too long into those murky, unmoving depths. A stain on the land, a seeping hole in the leprous skin of the swamp, blue lights above the waters on a long summer's evening, and Apalachee mothers told their children

about the demons from the moon, the star-fall whisperers below
the water.

"At night there, something uncanny happens: the water burns."

Infinities away, the lion closed its sleepy eyes and opened them
and closed them again. And again. And again.

The world turns.

The water burns.

*My heart beat like a hammer, my arms wound around you tight, and
stars fell on Alabama . . . last night.*

Knuckles like a hammer on the door, flesh and bone on wood,
and "You do exactly like I told you," Mr. Jube says. Glistening
beads of sweat on his brow, sweat hanging like dew from the
end of his nose. "Tomorrow mornin', I'll go into Milligan and
buy you a whole *bag* of them green jellybeans."

And Dancy nods her head, but he doesn't see, is already
reaching for the doorknob with unsteady hands, and whoever it
is knocks again, harder than before, and the door shudders on
its hinges. She imagines that she's holding a crooked, long
hickory stick and carefully draws the number 95 in the sand at
the edge of the lake.

"Just hold your horses a goddamned minute," the old man
croaks, the knob turning in his hand, and he opens the door.

And Dancy sees the eyes and forgets all about the numbers, 95
erased with the toe of her boot, smooth sand like brown sugar,
and that's as far as she goes; there's nothing out there but the eyes,
twin balls of the deepest, the most vivid blue she's ever seen or
imagined, roiling, pupilless eyes that shine bright enough to blind
and somehow give off no light whatsoever. Blue eyes bulging from
the fabric of the night, and Mr. Jube takes a small, hesitant step
backwards and looks down at the floor between his feet.

Don't you scream now, girl, Dancy thinks in the old man's voice.
Don't you dare start screamin'. She tries to look away, look down

like Mr. Jube did, tries to bow her head so there's nothing but her shoes and the floorboards, the spilled jellybeans, but she can't—not for all the tea in China, all the love of God—and her heart skips a beat as those blue eyes narrow down to suspicious, angry slits and glare past Mr. Jube directly at her.

"*Who's she*," the thing on the porch growls in a voice that is thunder and wildfire and the buzzing wings of poisonous red wasps. Movement in the darkness, and Dancy can see that there's more to it than the eyes, after all, that it's pointing towards her.

"She ain't no one," Mr. Jube says. "Least ways, no one you got to be concerned about."

"*You know the rules*," it growls, eyes swelling wide again, eyes big around as oranges, and the dark around them flutters for a moment and is still again.

"Yeah, I know she ain't supposed to be here. I know ain't *nobody* supposed to be here but me. But it just kinda happened, and there ain't no use worryin' over it now."

"*Dancy*," the thing purrs. "*Dancy Flammarion*," and the sudden, hot trickle down her thighs as she wets herself. She bites at her lower lip, bites hard until there's blood and it hurts too much to bite anymore, but she doesn't scream.

"She ain't gonna tell a single living soul what she's seein' here tonight," the old man says, and Dancy realizes that he's pleading for her life. "She knows better. She knows what would happen if she ever did."

"*Does she?*" it asks, blue eyes swirling, restless, disbelieving. "*Does she know the rules?*" But it stops pointing at her, and the jointed thing that isn't an arm melts back into the blackness.

"*The day you were born*," it says, and some of it flows across the threshold, sticky, tar-baby shreds of itself to lap about Mr. Jube's ankles. He takes a deep, hitching breath and stands absolutely still. "*There were tears the day you were born, Dancy Flammarion. There are tears in your mother's heart every time she looks at you.*"

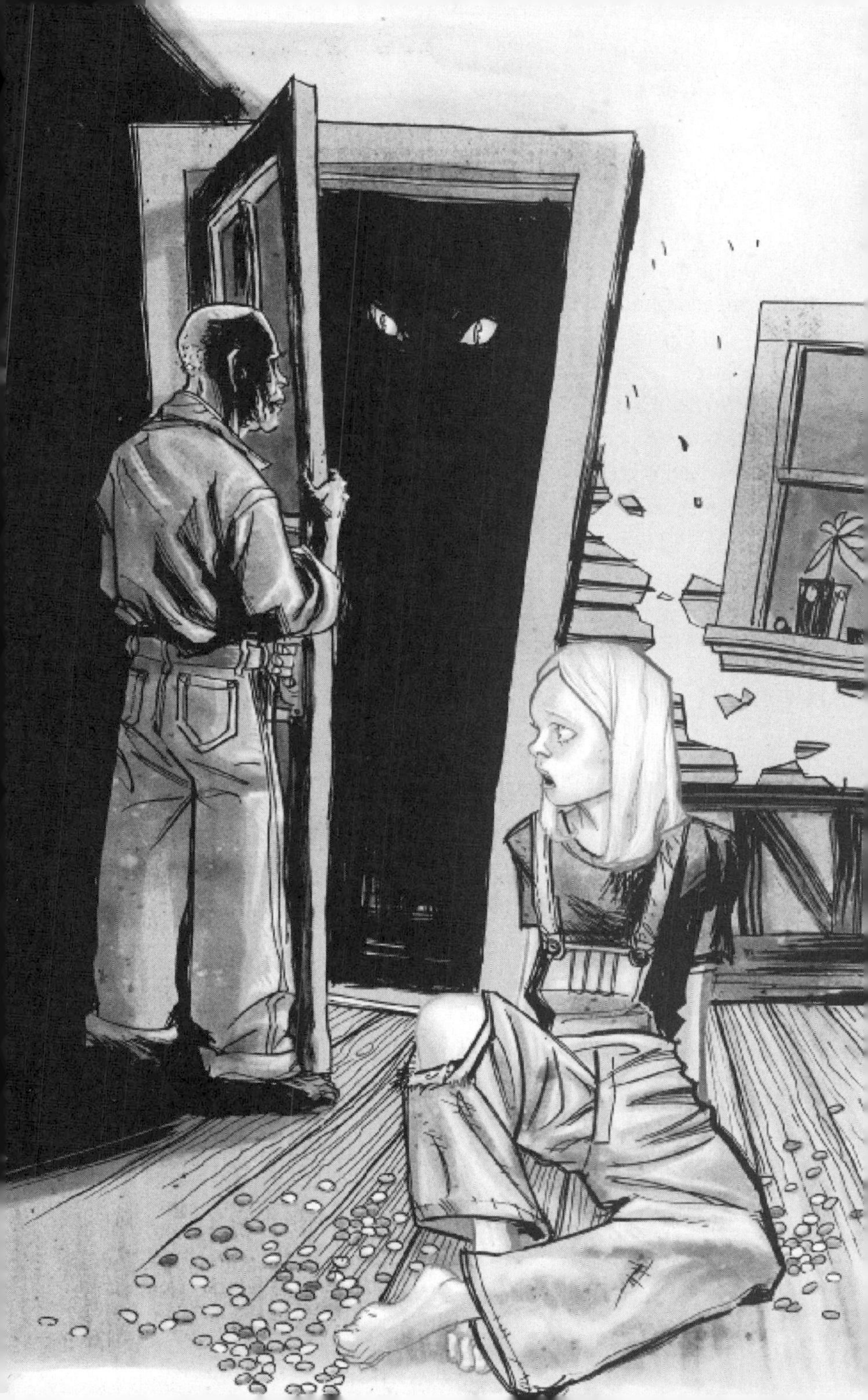

"I have the riddle," Mr. Jube says.

A black tendril wriggles noiselessly across the pine boards towards Dancy, its ragged tip end rising like the head of a coach-whip snake, serpent head pausing a few inches from her boots, and she smells dying fish and mud, peppermint and curdled milk.

"*But who's going to cry the day you leave?*" the thing at the door mutters in its thunderstorm, insect voice.

"You listenin'?" Mr. Jube says. "You know the rules. I only have to ask my riddle once."

The tendril hovers a moment longer near Dancy's left foot, indecisive, reluctant, and then it slips back across the floor, flows away and leaves behind a glistening slug trail on the rough wood.

"*Then ask me, old man. Ask me quick, before I forget the rules and take what I please.*"

The black puddle around Mr. Jube's feet shivers like jelly, and "You ain't never gonna get this one," he says, glances back at Dancy, and there's the thinnest ghost of a smile on his lips. "When the sun's done flickered out and the seas freeze up hard as gravestones, you still ain't gonna get this one here."

"*Ask me the riddle. Why does the crow fly in the woods? What kind of bushes do rabbits sit under when the rain comes?*"

Mr. Jube raises his head and stares directly into those huge and bottomless blue eyes, and when he speaks, his voice is calm and sure.

"The man who made me, never used me. The man who bought me, never used me. The man who used me, never saw me."

A gust of cold and stinking air through the open doorway and the lantern on the table glows brighter for a moment, its small flame swelling, flickering against the chill, as the blackness uncoils from about Mr. Jube's ankles. Pouring itself backwards, slow as syrup, and the eyes narrow once more down to angry, hating slits.

"Maybe next time," Mr. Jube says, and he looks down at the cabin floor again. "I can tell you're gettin' smarter. I'm gonna shut the door now," and he does, easy as that, closes it gently, latch click, and they're alone. The old black man and the albino girl, and she doesn't say a word, waits until he turns his back on the night and whatever it hides, and sits down across the table from her.

"You got blood on your face, child," he says. "Looks like you done bit a hole clean through your bottom lip. Just let me get my breath, and I'll see about it."

"I'm all right," Dancy says. "It don't hurt," not the truth but the pain seems small and far away. She stares at the checkerboard, the candy strewn at her feet, the kerosene lantern flame no larger or brighter than any lantern flame ought to be.

"You got your questions, too. I know that."

"What if it had known that riddle? What if it had guessed—"

"No," Mr. Jube says, interrupting her, and he shakes his head slowly and rubs at his beard. "I said I know you got questions. I *didn't* say I got answers. Hell, there ain't no answers for things like this, Dancy. That's just somethin' you gotta learn. Ain't everything in the world got a *what* and a *why* for the askin'."

"But it knew my name. It looked at me and knew my name."

"Well, you try not to think about that too much. It don't mean nothin'. It probably don't mean nothin' at all."

And outside the cabin by the lake at the end of Wampee Creek, the summer night mumbles uneasily to itself in the dark tongue of pine needles and cypress leaves, cricket whispers and the mournful call of owls. The waxing sliver of moon rises higher and casts a thin, pale glow across the water, and in a little while the surface of the pool has grown still and flat again, and the world rolls on towards morning.

Waycross

"Rise and shine, Snow White," the Gynander growls, and so
the albino girl slowly opens her pink eyes, the dream of her dead
mother and sunlight and the sheltering sky dissolving to the bare
earth and meat-rot stink of the cellar.

Go back to sleep, and I'll be home again, she thinks. *Close my
eyes, and none of this has ever happened.* Not the truth, nothing
like the truth, but cold comfort better than no comfort at all
in this hole behind the place where the monster sleeps during
the day. Dancy blinks at the darkness, licks her dry, chapped
lips, and tries hard to remember the story her mother was
telling her in the dream. Lion's den, whale belly, fiery-furnace
Bible story, but all the words and names running together in
her head, the pain and numbness in her wrists and ankles more
real, and the dream growing smaller and farther away with
every beat of her heart.

The red thing crouched somewhere at the other side of the
cellar makes a soft, wet sound and strikes a match to light the
hurricane lamp gripped in the long, raw fingers of its left hand.
Dancy closes her eyes, because the angel has warned her never
to look at its face until after it puts on one of the skins hanging
from the rusted steel hooks set into the ceiling of the cellar. All
those blind and shriveled hides like deflated people, deflated
animals, and it has promised Dancy that some day very soon
she'll hang there, too, one more hollow face, one more mask for
it to wear.

"What day . . . What day is it?" Dancy whispers, hard to talk because her throat's so dry, hard to even swallow, and her tongue feels swollen. "How long have I been down here?"

"Why?" the Gynander asks her. "What difference does it make?"

"No difference," Dancy croaks. "I just wanted to know."

"You got some place to be? You got someone else to kill?"

"I just wanted to know what day it is."

"It isn't any day. It's *night.*"

Yellow-orange lantern light getting in through Dancy's eyelids, warm light and cold shadows, and she squeezes them shut tighter, turns her head to one side so her face is pressed against the hard dirt floor. Not taking any chances because she promised she wouldn't ever look, and if she starts lying to the angel he might stop coming to her.

"Sooner or later, you're gonna *have* to take a look at me, Dancy Flammarion," the Gynander says and laughs its bone-shard, thistle laugh. "You're gonna have to open them rabbity little eyes of yours and have a good long look, before we're done."

"I was having a dream. You woke me up. Go away so I can go back to sleep. Kill me, or go away."

"You're already dead, child. Ain't you figured that out yet? You been dead since the day you came looking for me."

Footsteps, then, the heavy, stumbling sounds its splayed feet make against the hard-packed floor, and the clank and clatter of the hooks as it riffles through the hides, deciding what to wear.

"Kill me, or go away," Dancy says again, gets dirt in her mouth and spits it back out.

"Dead as a doornail," it purrs. "Dead as a dodo. Dead as I want you to be," and Dancy tries not to hear what comes next, the dry, stretching noises it makes stuffing itself into the skin suit it's chosen from one of the hooks. If her hands were free she could cover her ears; if they weren't tied together behind her back with nylon rope she could shove her fingers deep into her ears and maybe block it out.

"You can open your eyes now," the Gynander says. "I'm decent."

"Kill me," Dancy says, not opening her eyes.

"Why do you keep saying that? You don't want to die. When people want to die, when they *really* want to die, they get a certain smell about them, a certain brittle *incense*. You, you smell like someone who wants to live."

"I failed, and now I want this all to end."

"See, now *that's* the truth," the Gynander says, and there's a ragged zipping-up sort of sound as it seals the skin closed around itself. "You done let that angel of yours down, and you're ashamed, and you're scared, and you sure as hell don't want what you got coming to you. But you *still* don't want to die."

Dancy turns her head and opens her eyes, and now the thing is squatting there in front of her, holding the kerosene lamp close to its face. Borrowed skin stitched together from dead men and dogs, strips of diamond-backed snake hide, and it pokes at her right shoulder with one long black claw.

"This angel, he got hisself a name?"

"I don't know," Dancy says, though she knows well enough that all angels have names. "He's never told me his name."

"Must be one bad motherfucker, he gotta send little albino bitches out to do his dirty work. Must be one mean-ass son of a whore."

When it talks, the Gynander's lips don't move, but its chin jiggles loosely, and its blue-gray cheeks bulge a little. Where its eyes should be there's nothing at all, blackness to put midnight at the bottom of the sea to shame. And Dancy knows about eyes, windows to the soul, so she looks at the lamp instead.

"Maybe he ain't no angel. You ever stop and let yourself think about that, Dancy? Maybe he's a monster, too."

When she doesn't answer, it pokes her again, harder than before, drawing blood with its ebony claw; warm crimson trickle across her white shoulder, precious drops of her life wasted on the cellar floor, and she stares deep into the flame trapped inside the glass chimney. Her mother's face hidden in there somewhere, and a thousand summer-bright days, and the sword her angel carries to divide the truth from lies.

"Maybe you got it turned round backwards," the Gynander says and sets the lamp down on the floor. "Maybe what you *think* you know, you don't know at all."

"I knew right where to find you, didn't I?" Dancy asks it, speaking very quietly and not taking her eyes off the lamp.

"Well, yeah, now, that's a fact. But someone like me, you know how it is. Someone like me always has enemies. Besides the angels, I mean. And word gets around, no matter how careful—"

"Are you *afraid* to kill me? Is that it?"

And there's a loud and sudden flutter from the Gynander's chest, then, like a dozen mockingbirds sewn up in there and wanting out, frantic wings beating against that leather husk. It leans closer, scalding carrion breath and the fainter smell of alcohol, the eager *snik snik snik* of its sharp white teeth, but Dancy keeps staring into the flickering heart of the hurricane lamp.

"Someone like you," she says, "needs to know who its enemies are. Besides the angels, I mean."

The Gynander hisses through its teeth and slips a hand around her throat, its palm rough as sandpaper, its needle claws spilling more of her blood.

"Patience, Snow White," it sneers. "You'll be dead a long, long time. I'll wear your pretty alabaster skin to a thousand slaughters, and your soul will watch from Hell."

"Yeah," Dancy says. "I'm starting to think you're gonna talk me to death," and she smiles for the beast, shuts her eyes, and the afterimage of the lamp flame bobs and swirls orange in the dark behind her lids.

"You're still alive 'cause I still got things to *show* you, girl," the Gynander growls. "Things those fuckers, those *angels*, ain't ever bothered with, 'cause they don't want you to know how it is. But if you're gonna fight with monsters, if you're gonna play saint and martyr for cowards that send children to do their killing, you're gonna have to see it *all*."

Its grip on her throat tightens, only a little more pressure to crush her windpipe, a careless flick of those claws to slice her throat, and for a moment Dancy thinks maybe she's won after all.

"This whole goddamn world is *my* enemy," the thing says. "Mine and yours both, Dancy Flammarion."

And then it releases her, takes the lamp and leaves her alive, alone, not even capable of taunting a king of butchers into taking her life. Dancy keeps her eyes closed until she hears the trapdoor slam shut and latch, until she's sure she's alone again, and then she rolls over onto her back and stares up at the blackness that may as well go on forever.

After the things that happened in Bainbridge, Dancy hitched the long asphalt ribbon of US 84 to Thomasville and Valdosta, following the highway on to Waycross. Through the swampy, cypress-haunted south Georgia nights, hiding her skin and her pink eyes from the blazing June sun when she could, hiding herself from sunburn and melanoma and blindness. Catching rides with truckers and college students, farmers and salesmen, rides whenever she was lucky and found a driver who didn't think she looked too strange to pick up, maybe even strange enough to be dangerous or contagious. And when she was unlucky, Dancy walked.

The last few miles, gravel and sandy red-dirt back roads between Waycross and the vast Okefenokee wilderness, all of those unlucky, *all* of those on foot. She left the concrete-and-steel shade of the viaduct almost two hours before sunset, because the angel said she should. This time it wouldn't be like Bainbridge or the Texaco Station. This time there would be sentries, and this time she was expected. Walking right down the middle of the road because the weedy ditches on either side made her nervous; anything could be hiding in those thickets of honeysuckle and blackberry briars, anything hungry, anything terrible, anything at all. Waiting patiently for her beneath the deepening pine and magnolia shadows, and Dancy carried the old carving knife she usually kept tucked way down at the bottom of her duffel bag, held it gripped in her right hand and watched the close and darkening woods.

When the blackbird flapped noisily out of the twilight sky and landed on the dusty road in front of her, Dancy stopped and stared at it apprehensively. Scarlet splotches on its wings like fresh blood or poisonous berries, and the bird looked warily back at her.

"Oh Jesus, you gotta be pullin' my leg," the blackbird said and frowned at her.

"What's your problem, bird?" Dancy asked, gripping the knife a little tighter than before.

"I mean, we wasn't expecting no goddamn St. George on his big white horse or nothin', but for crying out loud."

"You knew I was coming here tonight?" she asked the bird and glanced anxiously at the trees, the sky, wondering who else might know.

"Look, girlie, do you have any idea what's waitin' for you at the end of this here road? Do you even have the foggiest—"

"This is where he sent me. I go where my angel sends me."

The blackbird cocked its head to one side and blinked at her.

"Oh Lord and butter," the bird said.

"I go where my angel tells me. He shows me what I need to know."

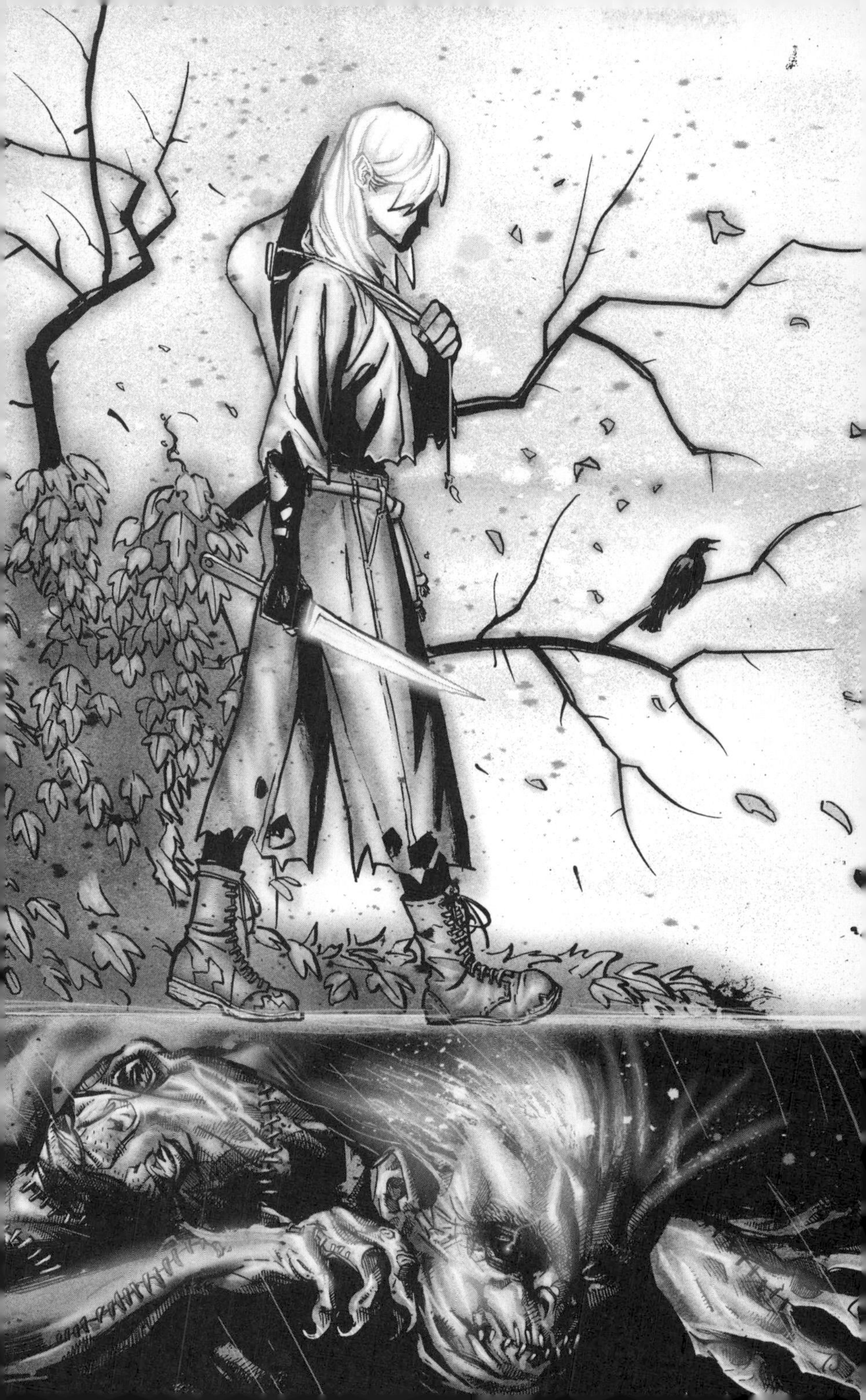

The blackbird glanced back over the red patch on its shoulder at the place where the dirt road turned sharply, disappearing into a towering cathedral of kudzu vines. It ruffled its feathers and shook its head.

"Yeah, well, this time I think somebody up there musta goofed. So you just turn yourself right around and get a wiggle on before anyone notices."

"Are you testing me? Is this a temptation? Did the monsters send you?"

"*What?*" the bird squawked indignantly and hopped a few inches closer to Dancy; she raised her carving knife and took one step backwards.

"Are you trying to stop me, bird? Is that what you're doing?"

"No. I'm trying to *save* your dumb ass, you simple twit."

"Nobody can save me," Dancy said and looked down at her knife. In the half-light, the rust on the blade looked like old dried blood. "Maybe once, a long, long time ago, but no one can save me now. That's not the way this story ends."

"Go *home*, little girl," the bird said and hopped closer. "Run away home before it smells you and comes lookin' for its supper."

"I don't have a home. I go where the angel tells me to go, and he told me to come here. He said there was something terrible hiding out here, something even the birds of the air and the beasts of the field are scared of, something I have to stop."

"With *what*? That old knife there?"

"Did you call me here, blackbird?"

"Hell, no," the bird cawed at her, angry, and glanced over its shoulder again. "Sure, we been prayin' for someone, but not a crazy albino kid with a butcher knife."

"I have to hurry now," Dancy said. "I don't have time to talk anymore. It's getting dark."

The bird stared up at her for a moment, and Dancy stared back at it, waiting for whatever was coming next, whatever she was meant to do or say, whatever the bird was there for.

"Jesus, you're really goin' through with this," it said finally, and she nodded. The blackbird sighed a very small, exasperated sigh and pecked once at the thick dust between its feet.

"Follow the road, past that kudzu patch there, and the old well, all the way down to—"

"I know where I'm going, bird," Dancy said and shifted the weight of her duffel bag on her shoulder.

"Of course you do. Your *angel* told you."

"The old blue trailer at the end of the road," Dancy whispered. "The blue house trailer with three old refrigerators in the front yard." In the trees, fireflies had begun to wink on and off, off and on, a thousand yellow-green beacons against the gathering night. "Three refrigerators and a broken-down truck."

"Then you best shove in your clutch, girl. And don't think for a minute that they don't know you're comin'. They know everything. They know the number of stars in the heavens and how many days left till the end of time."

"This is what I do," she told the bird and stepped past him, following the road that led to the blackness coiled like a jealous, ancient serpent beneath the summer sky.

Sometime later, when the Gynander finally comes back to her, it's carrying a small wooden box that it holds out for Dancy to see. Wood like sweet, polished chocolate and an intricate design worked into the lid—a perfect circle filled in with a riot of intersecting lines to form a dozen or more triangles, and on either side of the circle a waning or waxing half-moon sickle. She blinks at the box in the unsteady lantern light, wondering if the design is supposed to mean something to her, if the monster thinks that it will.

"Pretty," Dancy says without enthusiasm. "It's a pretty box."

The Gynander makes a hollow, grumbling sound in its throat, and the dead skin hiding its true face twitches slightly.

"You never saw that before?" it asks her and taps at the very center of the circular design with the tip of one claw. "You never saw that anywhere else?"

"No. Can I please have a drink of water?"

"Your *angel* never showed it to you?"

"No," Dancy says again, giving up on the water, and she goes back to staring at the rooty ceiling of the cellar. "I never saw anything like that before. Is it some sort of hex sign or something? My grandma knew a few of those. She's dead—"

"But you've never seen it before?"

"That's what I said."

The Gynander sits down in the dirt beside her, sets the lamp nearby, and she can feel the black holes where its eyes should be watching her, wary nothingness peering suspiciously out from the slits in its mask.

"This box belonged to Sinethella."

"Who?"

"The woman that you *killed* last night," the Gynander growls, beginning to sound angry again.

"I didn't kill a woman," Dancy says confidently. "I don't kill people."

"It's carved from a type of African cedar tree that's been extinct for two thousand years," the Gynander says, ignoring Dancy, and its crackling voice makes her think of dry autumn leaves and fire. "And she carried this box for eleven millennia. You got any idea what that means, child?"

"That she was a lot older than she looked," Dancy replies, and the Gynander grunts and puts the box down roughly on her chest. Heavy for its size, and cold, like a small block of ice, and suddenly the musty cellar air smells like spices—cinnamon, basil, sage, a few others that Dancy doesn't immediately recognize or has never smelled before.

"Get that thing off me," she tells the monster. "Whatever it is, I don't want it touching me. It isn't clean."

"Next to Sinethella," the Gynander says, "I'm nothing, nothing at all. Next to her, I'm just a carny freak. So why did you come for me instead of her?"

"I go where my angel leads me. He shows me—"

"In a moment, Dancy Flammarion, I'm going to open up this box here and show you what's inside."

"Get it off me. It stinks."

The Gynander grunts, then leans very close to Dancy and sniffs at her; something almost like a tongue, the dark, unhealthy color of indigo or poke-salad berries, darts out from between its shriveled lips and tastes the cellar air.

"That's sorta the pot callin' the kettle black, don't you think? When's the last time *you* had a bath, Snow White?"

And Dancy shuts her eyes, praying that her angel will come, after all, that he'll appear in a whirling storm of white, white feathers and hurricane wind and take her away from this awful place. She imagines herself in his arms, flying high above the swamps and pine barrens, safe in the velvet and starlight spaces between the moon and earth. I've done my best, she thinks, trying not to imagine what's waiting for her inside the freezing wooden box pressing painfully down on her chest. *I've done my best, and none of these things can ever touch my immortal soul.*

"When men still huddled in their own filth," the Gynander says, "and worshiped the sun because they were too afraid to face the night, she walked the wide world, and nobody and nothin' stood against her. She was a goddess, almost."

"I saw her with my own eyes," Dancy whispers. "I saw exactly what she was."

"You saw what you were told to see."

Sailing with her angel high above the winding black waters of the Okefenokee, above the booming voices of bull alligators and the nervous ears of marsh rabbits, safe in his arms because she's done the best that she can do. And he would tell her that, and that she doesn't have to be strong anymore. Time now to lie down and die, finally, time to be with her grandmother and mother in Paradise, no more lonely roads, no more taunts for her pink eyes and alabaster skin, and no more monsters. The angel's wings would sound like redemption, and she might glance down between her feet to see the Gynander's blue house trailer blazing in the night. "It'll be nothing but ashes by morning," she'd say and the angel would smile and nod his head.

"The first time Sinethella brought this box to me, first time she opened it and let me have a peek inside, I thought that I would surely die. I thought my heart would burst."

There are no more monsters left in the world, the angel would say to her as they flew across the land, east towards the sea. *You don't have to be afraid anymore. You can rest now, Dancy.*

"She read me a poem, before she let me look inside," the Gynander says. "I never was much for poetry, but I still remember this one. Hell, I'll remember this one till the day I die."

She would ask her angel about the box, and he would tell her not to worry. The box was destroyed. Or lost in the swamp in some pool so deep only the catfish will ever see it. Or locked away forever in the inviolable vaults of Heaven.

"*But from my grave across my brow*," the Gynander whispers, "*plays no wind of healing now, and fire and ice within me fight, beneath the suffocating night.*"

Open your eyes, Dancy, the angel says, and she does, not afraid of falling anymore, and the Gynander opens the box sitting on her chest. Far, far away, there's a sound like women crying, and the ebony and scarlet light that spills from the cedar box wraps

Dancy tight in its searing, squirming tendrils, and slowly, bit by bit, drags her away.

Dancy walked through the long, dark tunnel formed by the strangling kudzu vines, the broad green leaves muffling her footsteps, the heavy lavender flowers turning the air to sugar. She moved as quickly as she dared, wishing now that the black-bird had come with her, wishing she'd gotten an earlier start, and then there would still be a few bright shafts of late afternoon sunlight to pierce the tunnel of vines. Surrounded by the droning scream of cicadas, the songs of crickets and small peeping frogs hidden in amongst the rotten branches and trunks of the oaks that the kudzu had taken long ago for its skeleton, she counted her paces, like rosary beads, something to mark distance and occupy her mind, something to keep her focused and moving. No more than a hundred feet from one end to the next, a hundred feet at the most, but it might as well have been a mile. And halfway through, she reached a spot where the air was as cold as a January morning, air so cold her breath fogged, and Dancy jumped backwards, hugging herself and shivering.

Too late, she thought. *It knows I'm coming now*, realizing that the forest around her had gone completely quiet, not one insect or amphibian voice, no twilight birdsongs left to break the sudden silence.

Reluctantly, she held a hand out, penetrating the frigid curtain of air again, a cold that could burn, that could freeze living flesh to stone; she drew a deep breath and stepped quickly through it.

Beyond the vines, the blue house trailer was sitting there alone in a small weedy clearing, just like she'd seen it in her dreams, just exactly the way the angel had shown it to her. Light spilled from the windows and the door standing wide open like a welcome sign—*Come on in. I've been waiting for you, Dancy Flammarion.*

She set her duffel bag down on the ground and looked first at her knife and then back to the blue trailer. Even the shimmering, mewling things she'd faced back in Bainbridge, even they were afraid of *this* haunted place, something so terrible inside those aluminum walls that even boogeymen and goblins were afraid to whisper its name. Dancy glanced up at the summer sky, hoping the angel might be there, watching over her, but there were only a few dim and disinterested stars.

Well, what are you waiting on? the trailer seemed to whisper.

"Nothing," she said. "I'm not waiting on anything."

She walked past the three refrigerators, the burned-out carcass of the old Ford pickup, and climbed the cinder-block steps to stand in the open doorway. For a moment, the light was so bright that she thought it might blind her, might shine straight into her head and burn her brain away, and Dancy squinted through the tears streaming from the corners of her eyes. Then the light seemed to ebb, dimming enough that she could make out the shoddy confusion of furniture crammed into the trailer: a sofa missing all its cushions, a recliner the color of Spanish moss, and a coffee table buried beneath dirty plates, magazines, chicken bones, beer cans, and overflowing ashtrays. A woman in a yellow raincoat was sitting in the recliner, watching Dancy and smiling. Her eyes were very green and pupilless, a statue's jade-carved eyes, and her shaggy black hair fell about her round face in tangled curls.

"Hello there, Dancy," she said. "We were beginning to think that you wouldn't make it."

"Who are you?" Dancy asked, confused, and raised her knife so she was sure the woman could see it. "You're not supposed to be here. No one's supposed to be here but—"

"I'm not? Well, someone should have told me."

The woman stood up, slipping gracefully, slowly, from the gray recliner, her bare feet on the linoleum floor, and Dancy could see she wasn't wearing anything under the coat.

"Not exactly what you were expecting, am I?" she said, sounding pleased with herself, and took a single step towards Dancy. Beneath the bright trailer lights, her bare olive skin glinted wetly, skin as smooth and perfect as oil on deep, still water, and "Stop," Dancy warned her and jabbed the knife at the air between herself and the woman.

"No one here wants to hurt you," she said and smiled wider so that Dancy could see her long sharp teeth.

"I didn't come for you," Dancy said, trying hard to hide the tremble in her voice, because she knew the woman wanted her to be afraid. "I don't even know who you are."

"But I know who *you* are, Dancy. News travels fast these days. I know all about what you did in Bainbridge, and I know what you came here to do tonight."

"Don't make me hurt you, too."

"No one has to get hurt. Put the knife down, and we can talk."

"You're just here to distract me, so *it* can run, so it can escape, and then I'll have to find it all over again."

The woman nodded and looked up at the low ceiling of the trailer, her green eyes staring directly into the flood of white light pouring down into the tiny room.

"You have a hole inside you," she said, her smile beginning to fade. "Where your heart should be, there's a hole so awfully deep and wide, an abyss in your soul."

"That's not true," Dancy whispered.

"Yes, it is. You've lost everything, haven't you? There's nothing left in the world that you love and nothing that loves you."

And Dancy almost turned and ran, then, back down the cinder-block steps into the arms of the night, not prepared for this strange woman and her strange, sad voice, the secret things she had no right to know or ever say out loud. Not fair, the angel leaving this part out, not fair, when she's always done everything he asked of her.

"You think that *he* loves you?" the woman asked. "He doesn't. Angels love no one but themselves. They're bitter, selfish things, every one of them."

"Shut up."

"But it's the truth, dear. Cross my heart. Angels are nothing but spiteful—"

"I said to *shut up.*"

The woman narrowed her eyes, still staring up at the ceiling, peering into the light reflecting off her glossy skin.

"You've become their willing puppet, their doll," she sighed. "And, like the man said, they have made your life no more than a tale told by an idiot, full of sound and fury, signifying nothing. Nothing whatsoever."

Dancy gripped the carving knife and took a hesitant step towards the woman.

"You're a liar," she said. "You don't have any idea what you're talking about."

"Oh, but I *do*," the woman replied, lowering her head and turning to gaze at Dancy with those startling, unreal eyes. "I know so very many things. I can show you, if you want to see. I can show you the faces of God, the moment you will die, the dark places behind the stars," and she shrugged off the yellow raincoat, and it slipped to the linoleum floor.

Where her breasts should have been there were wriggling, tentacled masses instead, like the fiery heads of sea anemones, surrounding hungry, toothless mouths.

"There is almost no end to the things I can show you," the woman said. "Unless you're too afraid to see."

Dancy screamed and lunged towards the naked woman, all of her confusion and anger and disgust, all of her fear, flashing like steam to blind, forward momentum, and she swung the rusty knife, slashing the woman's throat open a couple of inches above her collarbones. The sudden, bright spray of blood across Dancy's

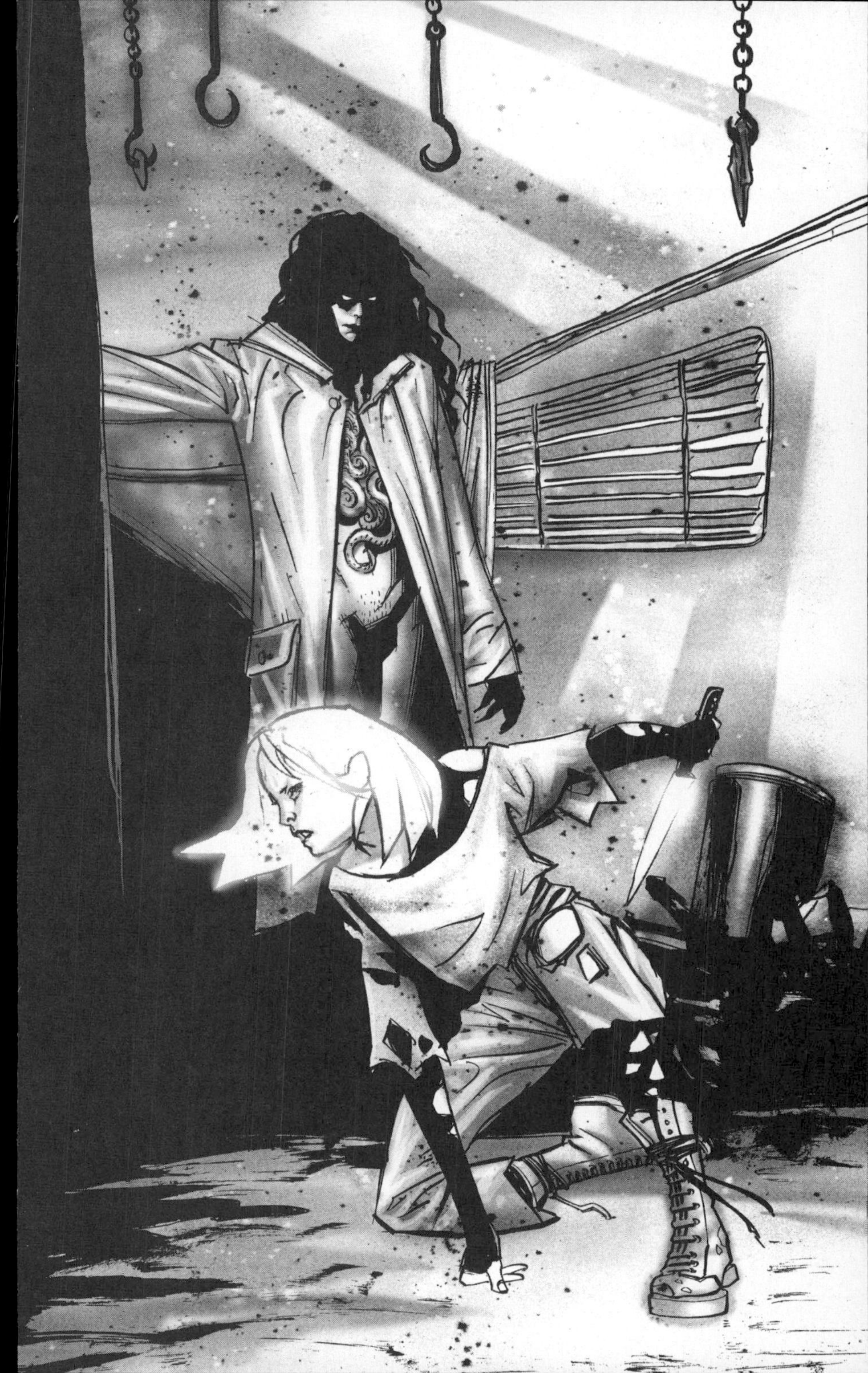

face was as cold as water drawn from a deep well, and she gasped and retreated to the door of the trailer. The knife slid from her hand and clattered against the aluminum threshold.

"You *cut* me," the woman sputtered, dismayed, and now there was blood trickling from her lips, too, blood to stain those sharp teeth pink and scarlet. Her green eyes had gone wide, swollen with surprise and pain, and she put one hand over the gash in her throat, as if to try and hide the wound hemorrhaging in time to her heart.

"You did it," she said. "You really fucking did it," and then the tentacles on her chest stopped wriggling, and she crumpled to the floor beside the recliner.

"Why didn't you tell me?" Dancy asked the angel, even though she knew it probably wasn't listening. "Why didn't you tell me she would be here, too?"

The woman's body shuddered violently and then grew still, lying on top of the discarded raincoat, her blood spreading out across the floor like a living stain. The white light from the ceiling began to dim and, a moment later, winked out altogether, so that Dancy was left standing in the dark, alone in the doorway of the trailer.

"What have you done to her?" the Gynander growled from somewhere close, somewhere in the yard behind Dancy, its heavy, plodding footsteps coming closer, and she murmured a silent, doubtful prayer and turned to face it.

Unafraid of falling, but falling nonetheless, as the living light from the wooden box ebbs and flows beneath her skin, between the convolutions of her brain. Collapsing into herself, that hole where her heart should be, that abyss in her soul, and all the things she's clung to for so long, the handholds clawed into the dry walls of her mind, melt beneath the corrosive, soothing voices of the light.

Where am I going? she asks, and the red and black tendrils squeezing her smaller and smaller, squeezing her away, reply in a hundred brilliant voices—*Inside*, they say, and *Down*, and *Back*, and finally, *Where the monsters come from.*

I don't have my knife, she says.

You won't need it, the light reassures her.

And Dancy watches herself, a white streak across a star-dappled sky, watches her long fall from the rolling deck of a sailing ship that burned and sank and rotted five hundred years ago. A sailor standing beside her curses, crosses himself, and points at Heaven.

"Did ye see it?" he asks in a terrified whisper, and Dancy can't tell him that she did and that it was only the husk of her body burning itself away, because now she's somewhere else, high above the masts and stays, and the boat is only a speck in the darkness below, stranded forever in a place where no wind blows and the sea is as still and flat as glass. *As idle as a painted ship, upon a painted ocean.*

Falling, not up or down, but falling farther in, and *Is there a bottom, or a top? Is there ever an end?*, she wonders, and *Yes*, the voices reply. *Yes and no, maybe and that depends.*

Depends on what?

On you, my dear. That depends on you.

And she stands on a rocky, windswept ledge, gray stone ground smooth and sheer by eons of frost and rain, and the mountains rise up around her until their jagged peaks scrape at the low-slung belly of the clouds. Below her is a long, narrow lake, black as pitch, and in the center of the lake, the ruins of a vast, shattered temple rise from its depths. There are things stranded out there among the ruins, nervous orange eyes watching the waters from broken spires and the safety of crumbling archways. Dancy can hear their small and timorous thoughts, no one desire among them but to reach the shore, to escape this cold, forgotten place— and they *would* swim, the shore an easy swim for even the weakest among them, but, from time to time, the black waters of the lake ripple, or a stream of bubbles rises suddenly to the surface, and there's no knowing what might be waiting down there. What might be hungry. What might have lain starving since time began.

"I want to go back now," Dancy says, shouting to be heard above the howling wind.

There's only one way back, the wind moans, speaking now for the light from the Gynander's box. *And that's straight on to the center.*

"The center of what?" Dancy shouts, and in a moment her voice has crossed the lake and echoed back to her, changed, mocking. *The center of when? Center of where? Of who?*

On the island of ruins, the orange-eyed things mutter ancient, half-remembered supplications and scuttle away into deeper shadows, Dancy's voice become the confirmation of their every waking nightmare, reverberating God voice to rain the incalculable weight of truth and sentence. And the wind sweeps her away like ash . . .

"What about her bush?" the orderly asks the nurse as the needle slips into Dancy's arm, and then he laughs.

"You're a sick fuck, Parker, you know that?" the nurse tells him, pulling the needle out again and quickly covering the tiny hole she's left with a cotton ball. "She's just a kid, for Christ's sake."

"Hey, it seems like a perfectly natural question to me. You don't see something like her every day of the week. Guys are curious about shit like that."

"Is that a fact?" the nurse asks the orderly, and she removes the cotton ball from Dancy's arm, stares for a moment at the single drop of crimson staining it.

"Yeah. Something like that."

"If you tell anyone, I swear to fucking—"

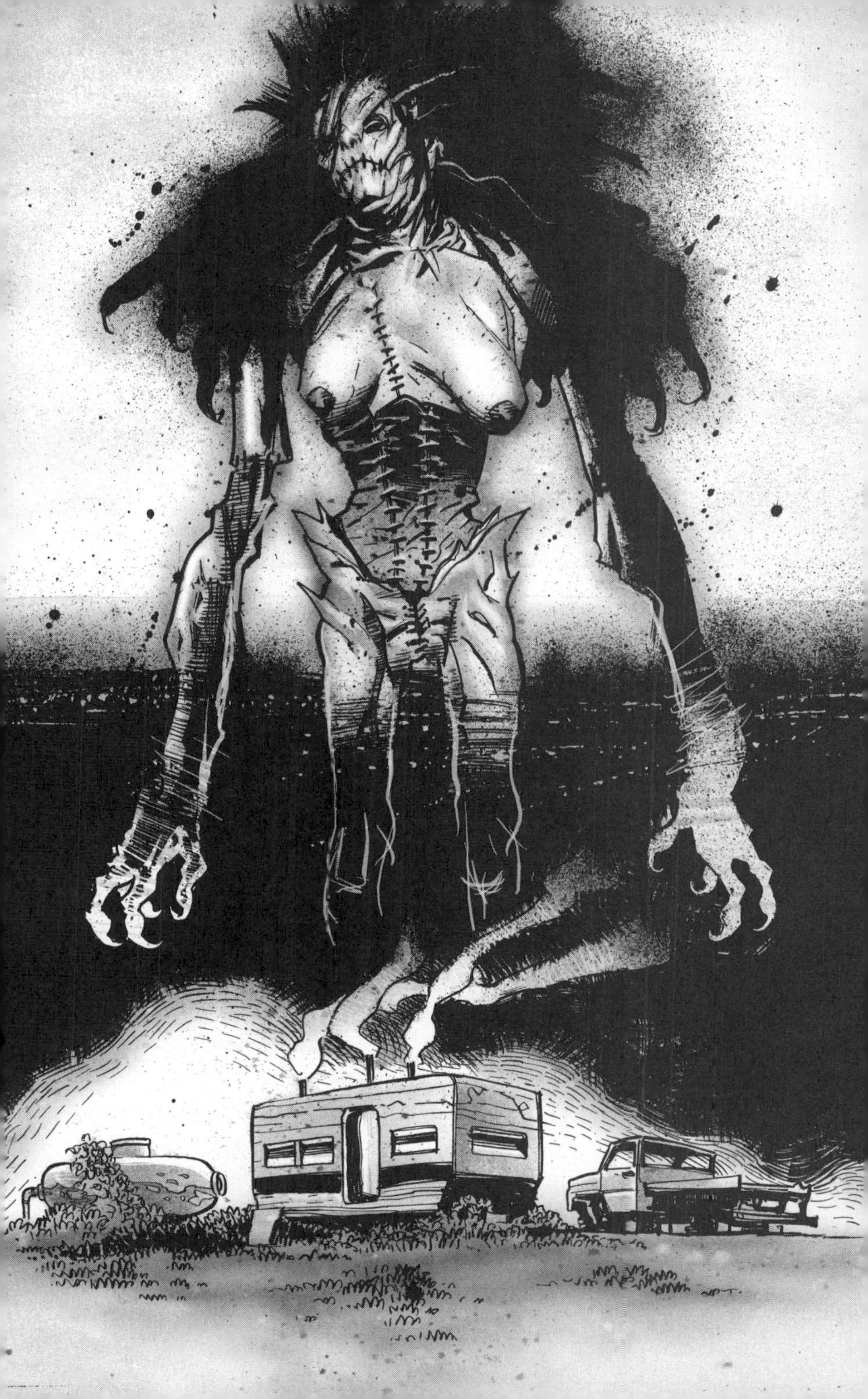

"Babe, this shit's between me and you. Not a peep, I swear."

"Jesus, I oughta have my head examined," the nurse whispers and drops the cotton ball and the syringe into a red plastic container labeled INFECTIOUS WASTE, then checks Dancy's restraints one by one until she's sure they're all secure.

"Is that me?" Dancy asks the lights, but they seem to have deserted her, left her alone with the nurse and the orderly in this haze of antiseptic stink and Thorazine.

"Is that me?"

The nurse lifts the hem of Dancy's hospital gown and, "There," she says and licks her lips. "Are you satisfied? Does that answer your question?" She sounds nervous and excited at the same time, and Dancy can see that she's smiling.

"Goddamn," the orderly mumbles, rubs at his chin and shakes his head. "Goddamn, that's a sight to see."

"Poor kid," the nurse says and lowers Dancy's gown again.

"Hey, wait a minute, I was gonna get some pictures," the orderly protests and laughs again.

"Fuck you, Parker," the nurse says.

"Anytime you're ready, baby."

"Go to hell."

And Dancy shuts her eyes, shuts out the white tile walls and fluorescent glare, pretends that she can't smell the nurse's flowery perfume or the orderly's sweat, that her arm doesn't ache from the needle and her head isn't swimming from the drugs.

Closing her eyes. Shutting one door and opening another.

The night air is very cold and smells like pine sap and dirt, night in the forest, and Dancy runs breathless and barefoot over sticks and stones and pine straw, has been running so long now that her feet are raw and bleeding. But she can hear the men on their horses getting closer, shouting to one another, the men and their hounds, and if she dares stop running they'll be on top of her in a heartbeat.

She stumbles and almost falls, cracks her left shoulder hard against the trunk of a tree and the force of the blow spins her completely around so that she's facing her pursuers, the few dark boughs left between them and her, and one of the dogs howls. The eager sound of something that knows it's almost won, that can taste her even before its jaws close around her throat.

The light from the box swirls about her like a nagging swarm of nocturnal insects, whirring black wings and shiny scarlet shells to get her moving again. Each step fresh agony now, but the pain in her feet and legs and chest is nothing next to her terror, the hammer of hooves and the baying hounds, the men with their guns and knives. Dancy cannot remember why they want her dead, what she might have done, if this is only some game or if it's justice; she can't remember when this night began or how long she's been running. But she knows that none of it will matter in the end, when they catch her, and then the earth drops suddenly away beneath her, and she's falling, really falling, the simple, helpless plummet of gravity. She crashes headlong through the branches of a deadfall and lands in a shallow, freezing stream.

The electric shock of cold water to rip the world around her open once again, the slow burn before it numbs her senseless, the fire before sleep and death to part the seams; she looks back to see the indistinct, frantic tumble of dog bodies already coming down the steep bank after her. Above them, the traitorous pines seem to part for the beautiful man on his tall black horse, his antique clothes, the torch in his hand as bright as the sun rising at midnight. His pale face is bruised with the anger and horror of everything he's seen and done, and everything he will see and do before the dawn.

"*Je l'ai trouvée!*" he shouts to the others. "*Dépêchez-vous!*"

Words Dancy doesn't know, but she *understands* them perfectly well, just the same.

"*La bête! Je l'ai trouvée!*"

And then she looks down at the reflection of the torchlight dancing in the icy, gurgling water, and her reflection there, as well, her albino's face melting in the flowing mirror, becoming the long snout and frightened, iridescent eyes of a wolf, melting again, and now the dead woman from the Gynander's trailer stares back at her. Dancy tries to stand, but she can't feel her legs anymore, and the dogs are almost on top of her, anyway.

"Is this me?" she asks the faces swirling in the stream. "Is this my face, too?" But this *when* and *where* slide smoothly out from beneath her before the light can reply, before snapping dog teeth tear her apart; caught up in the implosion again, swallowed whole by her own disintegration.

"They're all dead," the nurse says, and her white shoes squeak loud against the white floor. "Cops up in Milligan think maybe she had something to do with it."

"No shit?" the orderly says. He's standing by the window, looking out at the rain, drawing circles in the condensation with his index finger. Circles and circles inside circles. "Where the hell's Milligan?"

"If you don't know already, trust me, you don't want to know."

Far away, the beautiful man on his black horse fires a rifle into the night.

"How old were you then?" the psychiatrist asks Dancy, and she doesn't answer him right away, stares instead at the clock on the wall, wishing she could wait him out. Wishing there was that much time in the universe, but he has more time than she does. He keeps it nailed like Jesus to his office wall and doles it out in tiny paper cups, a mouthful at a time.

"Dancy, how old were you that night your mother took you to the fair?"

"Does it matter?" she asks him, and the psychiatrist raises his eyebrows and shrugs his bony old-man shoulders.

"It might," he says.

And the fair unfurls around her, giddy violence of colored lights and calliope wails, cotton-candy taffy air, sawdust air, barkers howling like drunken wolves, and the mechanical thunk and clank and wheeze of the rides. Her mother has an arm around her, holding her close as the sea of human bodies ebbs and surges about them, and Dancy thinks this must be Hell. Or Heaven. Too much of everything good and everything bad all shoved together into this tiny field, a deafening, swirling storm of laughter and screams; she wants to go home, but this is a birthday present, so she smiles and pretends that she isn't afraid.

"You didn't want to hurt your mother's feelings," the psychiatrist says and chews on the end of a yellow pencil. "You didn't want her to think you weren't having fun."

"Look, Dancy," her mother says. "Have you ever seen anything like that in your whole life?"

And the clown on stilts, tall as a tree, strides past them, wading stiffly through the crowd. He looks down as Dancy looks up, and the clown smiles at her, real smile behind his painted smile, but she doesn't smile back. She can see his shadow, the thing hiding in his shadow, its spidery-long legs and half-moon smile, its eyes like specks of molten lava burning their way out of its skull.

Dancy looks quickly down at the ground, trampled sawdust and mud, cigarette butts and a half-eaten candy apple, and "Get a load of her, will you?" a man says and laughs.

"Hey, girlie. You part of the freak show or what?"

"Course she is. She's one of the albinos. I saw the poster. They got a whole albino family. They got a boy that's half alligator and a stuffed cow with two heads. They got a Chinese 'maphrodite—"

"They ain't got no cow with two heads. That's a damn fake."

"Well, *she* ain't no fake, now is she?"

And then her mother is shoving a path through the crowd, towing Dancy after her, trying to get away from the two men, but they follow close behind.

"Slow up, lady," one of them shouts. "We just want to get a good look at her. We'll pay you."

"Yeah, that's right," the other one shouts, and now everyone is staring and pointing. "We'll pay. How much just to look? We ain't gonna touch."

The psychiatrist taps his pencil against his chin and helps Dancy watch the clock. "Were you mad at her afterwards, for taking you to the fair?" he asks.

"That was a long time ago," Dancy replies. "It was my birthday present."

He takes a deep breath and exhales slowly, makes a whistling sound between his front teeth.

"We never went anywhere, so she took me to the fair for my birthday."

"Did you know about freak shows, Dancy? Did your mother warn you about them before you went to the fair?"

"What's the difference between freaks and monsters?" she asks the psychiatrist.

"Monsters aren't real," he says. "That's the difference. Why? Do you think you're a monster? Has anyone ever told you that you're a monster?"

She doesn't answer him. In only five more minutes she can go back to her room and think about anything she wants, anything but fairs and grinning clowns on stilts and the way the two men stalked them through the crowd, anything but freaks and monsters. In the forest, the man fires his rifle again, and this time the shot tears a hole in the psychiatrist's face, so Dancy can see shattered bone and torn muscle, his sparkling silver teeth and the little metal gears and springs that move his tongue up and down. He drops the pencil, and it rolls underneath his desk; she wants to ask him if it hurts, being shot, having half your face blown off like that, but he hasn't stopped talking, too busy asking her questions to care if he's hurt.

"Have you ever been afraid that she took you there to get rid of you, to leave you with the freaks?"

And all the world goes white, a suffocating white where there is no sky and no earth, nothing to divide the one from the other, and the Arctic wind shrieks in her ears, and snow stings her bare skin. Not the top of the world, but somewhere very near it, a rocky scrap of land spanning a freezing sea, connecting continents in a far-off time of glaciers. Dancy wants to shut her eyes; then, at least, it would only be black, not this appalling, endless white, and she thinks about going to sleep, drifting down to someplace farther inside herself, the final still point in this implosion, down beyond the cold. But she knows that would mean death, in this place, this *when*, some mute instinct to keep her moving, answering to her empty belly when she only wants to be still.

"*Ce n'est pas un loup!*" the man on his horse shouts to the others in his company, and Dancy peers over her shoulder, but she can't see him anywhere. Nothing at all back there but the wind-blown snow, and she wonders how he could have possibly followed her to this time and place, when he won't even be born for another thirteen thousand years. The storm picks his voice apart and scatters it across the plains.

With the impatient wind at her back, hurrying her along, Dancy stumbles on ahead, helpless to do otherwise.

She finds the camp just past a line of high granite boulders, men and women huddled together in the lee of the stones, a ragged, starving bunch wrapped in bear hides. She smells them before she sees them—the soot of their small, smoky fires, the oily stink of their bodies, the faint death smell from the skins they wear. She slips between the boulders, sure footed, moving as quietly as she can, though they could never hear her coming over the wind. The wind that blows her own scent away, and she crouches above them and listens. The men clutching their long spears, the women clutching their children, and all eyes nervously watching the whiteout blur beyond the safety of the fires.

Dancy doesn't need to understand their language to read their minds, the red and ebony light coiled tight inside her head to translate their hushed words, their every fearful thought, to show her the hazy nightmares they've fashioned from the shadows and the wailing blizzard. They whisper about the strange creature that has been trailing them for days, tracking them across the ice, the red-eyed demon like a young girl carved from the snow itself. Their shaman mumbles warnings that they must have trespassed into some unholy place protected by this spirit of the storms, but most of the men ignore him. They've never come across any beast so dangerous it doesn't bleed.

Crouched there among the boulders, her teeth chattering, Dancy gazes up into the swirling snow. The light leaks out of her nostrils and twines itself in the air above her head like a dozen softly glowing serpents.

They will come for you soon, it says. *If you stay here, they'll find you and kill you.*

"Will they?" Dancy asks, too cold and hungry and tired to really care, one way or the other, and *Yes*, the light replies.

"Why? I can't hurt them. I couldn't hurt them if I wanted to."

The light breaks apart into a sudden shower of sparks, bright drops of fire that splash against each other and bounce off the edges of the boulders. In a moment, they come together again, and the woman from the Gynander's trailer, the woman in the yellow raincoat that she knows isn't a woman at all, steps out of the gloom and stands nearby, watching Dancy with her green eyes.

"It only matters that they are *afraid* of you," she says. "Maybe you could hurt them, and maybe you could not, but it only matters that they are afraid."

"I killed you," Dancy says. "You're dead. Go away."

"I only wanted you to see," the woman says and glances down at the camp below the boulders. "Sometimes we forget what we are and why we do the things we do. Sometimes we never learn."

"It won't make any difference," Dancy growls at her, and the woman smiles and nods her head. Her raincoat flutters and flaps loudly in the wind, and Dancy tries hard not to look at the things writhing on her bare chest.

"It might," the woman says. "Someday, when you can't kill the thing that frightens you. When there's nowhere left to run. Think of it as a gift."

"Why would you give *me* a gift?"

"Because you gave me one, Dancy Flammarion," and then the woman blows apart in the wind, and Dancy shivers and watches as the glittering pieces of her sail high into the winter sky and vanish.

"Is it over now?" Dancy asks the light, and in a moment it answers her. *That depends*, it says, and *Is it ever over?* it asks, but Dancy is already tumbling back the way she's come. Head over heels, ass over tits, and when she opens her eyes, an instant later, an eternity later, she's staring through the darkness at the ceiling of the Gynander's root cellar.

Dancy coughs and rolls over onto her left side, breathing against the stabbing, sharp pain in her chest, and there's the box sitting alone in the dust, its lid closed now. The dark, varnished wood glints dull in the orange light from the hurricane lantern hanging nearby, and whatever might have come out of the box has been locked away again. She looks up from the floor, past the drooping, empty husks on their hooks and the Gynander's workbenches, and the creature is watching her from the other side of the cellar.

"What did you see?" it asks her, and she catches a guarded hint of apprehension in its rough voice.

"What was I supposed to see?" Dancy asks back, and she coughs again. "What did you think I'd see?"

"That's not how it works. It's different for everyone."

"You wanted me to see things that would make me doubt what the angel tells me."

"It's different for everyone," the Gynander says again and draws the blade of a straight razor slowly across a long leather strap.

"But that's what you wanted, wasn't it? That's what you hoped I'd see, because that's what you saw when she showed you the box."

"I never talked to no angels. I made a point of that."

And Dancy realizes that the nylon ropes around her ankles and wrists are gone, and her knife is lying on the floor beside the box. She reaches for it, and the Gynander stops sharpening its razor and looks at her.

"Sinethella wanted to die, you know. She'd been wanting to die for ages," it says. "She'd heard what you did to them folks over in Bainbridge, and down there in Florida. I swear, child, you're like something come riding out of a Wild West movie, like goddamn Clint Eastwood, you are."

Dancy sits up, a little dizzy from lying down so long, and wipes the rusty blade of her carving knife on her jeans.

"Like in that one picture, *High Plains Drifter*, where that nameless stranger fella shows up acting all holier than thou. The whole town thinks they're using him, but turns out it's really the other way round. Turns out, maybe he's the most terrible thing there is, and maybe good's a whole lot worse thing to have after your ass than evil. Course, you have a name—"

"I haven't seen too many movies," Dancy says, though, in truth, she's never seen a single one. She glances from the Gynander to the wooden box to the lantern and back to the Gynander.

"I just want you to understand that she wasn't no two-bit, backwoods haint," it says and starts sharpening the straight razor again. "Not like me. I just want you to know ain't nothing happened here she didn't *want* to happen."

"Why did you untie me?"

"Why don't you try asking that angel of yours? I thought it had all the answers. Hell, I thought that angel of yours was all over the truth like flies on dog shit."

"She told you to let me go?"

The Gynander makes a sound like sighing and lays the leather strap aside, holds the silver razor up so it catches a little of the stray lantern light. Its stolen face sags and twitches slightly.

"Not exactly," it says. "Ain't nothing that easy, Snow White."

Dancy stands up, her legs stiff and aching, and she lifts the hurricane lantern off its nail.

"Then you want to die, too," she says.

"Not by a long sight, little girl. But I do like me some sport now and then. And Sinethella said you must be a goddamn force of nature, a regular shatterer of worlds, to do the things you been getting away with."

"What I saw in there," Dancy says, and she cautiously prods at the box with the toe of one shoe. "It doesn't make any difference. I know it was just a trick."

"Well, then what're you waiting for," the thing whispers from the lips of its shabby patchwork skin. "Show me what you got."

The fire crackles and roars at the night sky lightening slowly towards dawn. Dancy sits on a fallen log at the side of the red dirt road leading back to Waycross and watches as the spreading flames begin to devour the leafy walls of the kudzu tunnel.

"Well, I guess you showed me what for," the blackbird says. It's perched on the log next to her, the fire reflected in its beady eyes. "Maybe next time I'll keep my big mouth shut."

"You think there's ever gonna be a next time?" Dancy asks without looking away from the fire.

"Lord, I hope not," the birds squawks. "That was just, you know, a figure of speech."

"Oh. I see."

"Where you headed next?" the bird asks.

"I'm not sure."

"I thought maybe the angels—"

"They'll show me," Dancy says, and she slips the carving knife back into her duffel bag and pulls the drawstrings tight again. "When it's time, they'll show me."

And then neither of them says anything else for a while; they just sit there together on the fallen pine log, as the fire she started in the cellar behind the trailer burns and bleeds black smoke into the hyacinth sky.

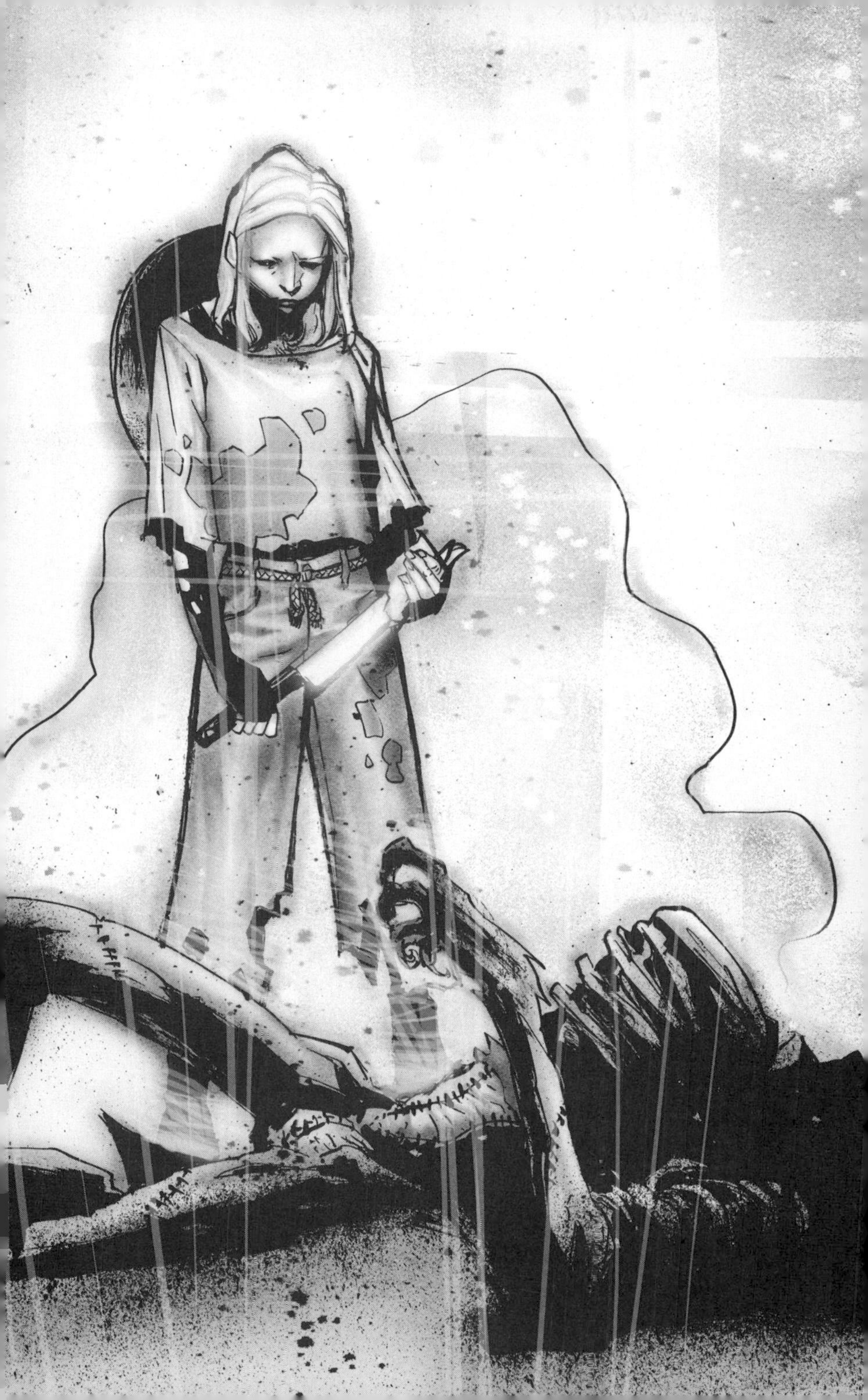

Alabaster

The albino girl, whose name is Dancy Flammarion, has walked a long way since the fire in Bainbridge, five nights ago. It rained all morning long, and the blue-gray clouds are still hanging sullen and low above the pines, obscuring the wide south Georgia sky. But she's grateful for the clouds, for anything that hides her from the blistering June sun. She's already thanked both St. George and St. Anthony the Abbot for sending her the clouds, because her grandmother taught her they were the patron saints of people suffering from skin diseases. Her grandmother taught her lots of things. The damp air smells like pine straw and the fat white toadstools growing along the side of the highway. Dancy knows not to eat those, not ever, no matter how hungry she gets. Her grandmother taught her about toadstools, too.

She stops, shifting the weight of her heavy old duffel bag from one shoulder to the other, the duffel bag and the black umbrella tied to it with hemp twine, and looks back the way she's just come. Sometimes it's hard to tell if the voices she hears are only inside her head or if they're coming from somewhere else. The highway glistens dark and wet and rough, like a cottonmouth moccasin that's just crawled out of the water. But there's no one and nothing back there that she can see, no one who might have spoken her name, so Dancy turns around and starts walking again.

It's what you don't *see that's almost always the worst,* her grandmother told her once. *It's what you don't see will drag you down one day, if you ain't careful.*

Dancy glances over her shoulder, and the angel is standing in the center of the highway, straddling the broken yellow dividing line. Its tattered muslin and silk robes are even blacker than the wet asphalt, and they flutter and flap in a fierce and holy wind that touches nothing else. The angel's four ebony wings are spread wide, and it holds a burning sword high above its four shimmering kaleidoscope faces, both skeletal hands gripped tightly around the weapon's silver hilt.

"I was starting to think maybe I'd lost you," Dancy says and turns to face the angel. She can hear the wind that swirls always about it, like hearing a freight train when you're only halfway across a trestle and there's no way to get off the tracks before it catches up with you, nowhere to go unless you want to fall, and that sound drowns out or silences the noises coming from the woods at the edge of the road.

And there's another sound, too, a rumble like thunder, but she knows that it isn't thunder.

"If I went any slower," she replies, "I'd just about be standing still."

The thunder sound again, and the roar of the angel's scalding wind, and Dancy squints into the blinding light that's begun to leak from its eight sapphire eyes.

"No, angel," she says quietly. "I ain't forgot about you. I ain't forgotten about any of it."

The angel shrieks and swings its burning sword in a long, slow arc, leaving behind bits of fire and ember, ash and cinders, and now the air smells more like burning pitch and charred flesh than it smells like pine trees and summer rain and poisonous toadstools.

"Oh, I think you can probably keep up," she says, and turns her back on the seraph.

And then there's only the dead, violated emptiness and the terrible silence that the angel always leaves behind when it goes.

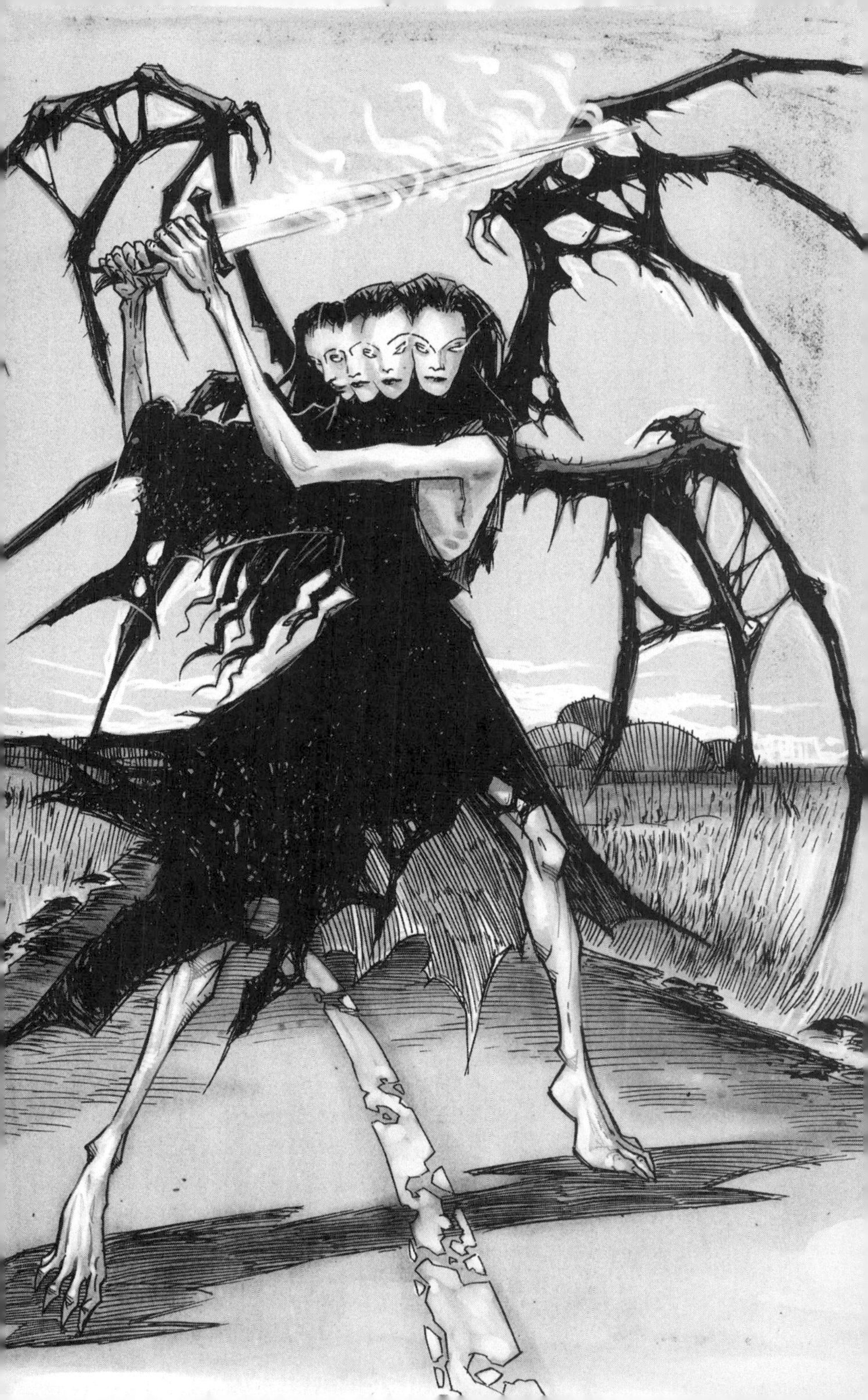

Very slowly, by hesitant degrees, all the murmuring forest noises return, and Dancy walks just a little faster than before; she's relieved when the high pines finally fall away on either side of the road and the land opens up, changing once more to farms and wild prairie. Pastures and cows, barbed-wire fences, and a small service station maybe a hundred yards or so farther down the highway, and Dancy wishes she had the money for a Coke. A Coke would be good, syrupy sweet and ice cold and bubbling on her tongue. But at least they won't charge her to use the toilet, and she can wash up a little and piss without having to worry about squatting in poison oak.

She doesn't look back at the woods again, the trees standing straight and tall on either side of the highway. That part of her life is over, lived and past and done with, one small stretch of road she only needed to walk once, and, besides, she knows the angel won't come to her again for days.

After the rain and the seraph's whirlwind, the afternoon is still and cool, and her boots seem very loud on the wet pavement. It only takes her a few more minutes to reach the service station, where an old man is sitting on a plastic milk crate beneath a corrugated tin awning. He waves to her, and Dancy waves back at him, then she tugs at the green canvas strap on her duffel bag because her shoulder's gone to sleep again.

There's a big plywood billboard beside the road, but it's not nearly so tall as the faded Texaco sign—that round placard dangling from a lamppost, a perfect black circle to contain its five-pointed red pentacle, that witch's symbol to keep out some great evil. Dancy already knows all about pentagrams, so she turns her attention to the billboard instead; it reads LIVE PANTHER—DEADLY MAN EATER in sloppy whitewash lettering.

She leaves the highway, skirting the edges of a wide orange-brown mud hole where the Texaco's parking lot and driveway begin, crunching across the white-gray limestone gravel strewn around the gasoline pumps. The old man is standing up now, digging about in a pocket of his overalls.

"How ya doin' there, sport?" he asks her, and his hand reappears with half a roll of wintergreen Certs.

"I'm fine," she says, not smiling because her shoulder hurts too much. "You got a bathroom I can use?"

"You gonna buy somethin'?" he asks and pops one of the Certs into his mouth. His teeth are stained yellow-brown, like turtle bones that have been lying for years at the bottom of a cypress spring.

"I don't have any money," she tells him.

"Hell," he says and sits back down on the plastic milk crate. "Well, I don't guess that makes no difference. The privy's right inside. But you better damn flush when you're done, you hear me? And don't you get piss on the seat."

Dancy nods her head, then stares at him until the old man leans back and blinks at her.

"You want somethin' else?"

"Do you really have a live panther?" she asks him, and the man arches both his eyebrows and grins, showing off his yellow-brown, tobacco-stained smile again.

"That's what the sign says, ain't it? Or cain't you read?"

"I can read," Dancy Flammarion replies and looks down at the toes of her boots. "I wouldn't have known to ask if I couldn't read."

"Then why'd you ask such a fool question for? You think I'm gonna put up a big ol' sign sayin' I got a live panther if I ain't?"

"Does it cost money to see it?"

"You better believe it does. I'll let you use the jake free of charge, 'cause it wouldn't be Christian to do otherwise, but a gander at that cat's gonna set you back three bucks, cold, hard cash."

"I don't have three dollars."

"Then I guess you ain't gonna be seein' my panther," the old man says, and he grins and offers her a Certs. She takes the candy from him and sets her duffel bag down on the gravel between them.

"How'd you get him?"

The old man rubs at the coarse salt-and-pepper stubble on his chin and slips what's left of the roll of Certs into the bib pocket of his overalls.

"You some kind of runaway or somethin'? You got people out lookin' for you, sport? You a druggie?"

"Is he in a cage?" she asks, matching his questions with a question of her own.

"He's a she," the old man grunts. "Course she's in a cage. What you *think* someone's gonna do with a panther? Keep it in a damned burlap sack?"

"No," she says. "How'd you say you caught him?"

"I didn't."

"Did someone else catch him for you?"

"It *ain't* no him. It's a *she*."

Dancy looks up at the old man and rolls the quickly shrinking piece of candy from one side of her mouth to the other and back again.

"You're some kinda albino, ain't you," the old man says, and he leans a little closer. He smells like sweat and Beech-Nut chewing tobacco, old cars and fried food.

"Yeah," she says and nods her head.

"Yep. I thought so. I used to have some rabbits had eyes like yours."

"Did you keep them in cages, too?"

"You keep rabbits in hutches, sport."

"What's the difference?"

The old man glares at her a moment and then sighs and jabs his thumb at the screen door. "The shitter's inside," he grumbles. "Right past the Pepsi cooler. And don't you forget to flush."

"Where do you keep him?" Dancy asks, looking past the old man at the closed screen door and the shadows waiting on the other side.

"That ain't exactly none of your business, not unless you got the three bucks, and you done told me you don't."

"I've seen some things," she says. "I've seen black bears, out in the swamps. I've seen gators, too, and once I saw a big ol' bobcat, but I've never seen a panther before. Is it the same thing as a cougar?"

"You gonna stand there talkin' all damn day long? I thought you needed to take a leak?"

Dancy shrugs her narrow shoulders and then looks away from the screen door, staring north and east down the long road to the place it finally vanishes, the point where the cloudy sky and the pastures collide.

"If any police show up askin' if I seen you, don't expect me to lie about it," the old man says. "You sure look like a runaway to me. No tellin' what kind of trouble you might be in."

"Thank you for the candy," she says and points at her duffel bag. "Is it okay if I leave that out here while I use your toilet? It's heavy."

"Don't make no difference to me," the man says. "But don't you forget to flush, you understand me?"

"Sure thing," Dancy says. "I understand," and she steps past him, climbs the four squeaky wooden steps up to the screen door and lets it bang shut. Inside, the musty air stinks of motor oil and dust, dirty rags and cigarette smoke, and the only light comes from the door and the flyspecked windows. The walls and floor are bare pine boards gone dark as rotten teeth, and a huge taxidermied bass hangs above the cash register. There are three short rows of canned goods, candy bars in brightly colored paper wrappers, oil and windshield wipers and transmission fluid, snack foods and mousetraps, bottles of Bayer aspirin and cherry-flavored Maalox.

There's a wall of hardware and fishing tackle. She finds the tiny restroom right where he said she would, and Dancy latches the door behind her.

The restroom is illuminated by a single, naked incandescent bulb hanging from the ceiling. Dancy squints up at it, raises her left hand for an eclipse, and then glances at her reflection in the smudgy mirror above a sink stained by decades of iron water. She isn't sure how long it's been since she's seen herself like that; not since sometime before Bainbridge, so more than a week, at least. Her white hair is still wet from the rain, wet and tangled like a drowned thing. A drowned rabbit that spent its whole short life trapped in a cage called a hutch, maybe, and she lowers her hand so the stark light spills down on her again.

The albino girl in the mirror lowers her hand, too, and stares back at Dancy with eyes that seem a lot older than Dancy's sixteen years. Eyes that might have been her grandmother's, if they were brown, or her mother's, if they were the easy green of magnolia leaves.

"You should wash your face," the albino girl in the mirror says. "You look like some sort of hobo."

"I didn't know it was so dirty," Dancy replies, embarrassed at her own raggedness, and almost adds, *I thought the rain would have washed it clean*, but then she thinks better of it.

There's a stingy violet-brown sliver of soap on the sink, but when she turns on the hot water, the knob marked H, she remembers how badly she has to pee and turns the water off again. She loosens her belt, and the pearl-handled straight razor tucked into the waistband of her jeans almost falls out onto the floor. She catches it and slips it into her back pocket. The razor, like the duffel bag, was her grandfather's, and he carried both of them when he fought the Nazis in Italy and France. Dancy didn't take many things out of her grandmother's cabin in Shrove Wood before she burned it, and the bodies inside, to the ground. But she took the straight razor, because the old man had shaved with it every morning, and it helped her remember him.

After she pees, Dancy wipes off the seat with a big wad of toilet paper, even though there's not a drop of urine on it anywhere. She drops the wad into the porcelain bowl, flushes, and the water swirls round and round like the hot wind that always swirls about her angel.

"You look like hell," the albino girl in the mirror says and frowns.

"I'm just tired, that's all. I didn't sleep very well last night," which is the truth. She slept a few hours in the back seat of an abandoned car that someone had stolen, stripped, and left in the woods, and her dreams were filled with images of the things she'd seen and done in Bainbridge and Shrove Wood, the angel and the things that want her dead and damned, the past and the present and the slippery, hungry future.

Dancy turns the hot water on again and uses the yellowish sliver of soap to wash her hands, her arms, her grimy face and neck. The soap smells like soap, but it also smells very faintly of black-eyed Susans and clover and sunshine, and she doesn't remember ever having smelled that sort of soap before. When she's done, she dries with brown paper towels from a chrome dispenser mounted on the wall. All that hot water's steamed up the mirror, and she uses another paper towel to wipe it clear again.

The albino girl is still there, watching Dancy from the other side.

"That's better," the girl in the mirror says. "Don't you think so?"

"It feels better," Dancy says, "if that's what you mean. And I like the way that soap smells."

"You know, I think you're running out of time," the girl in the mirror tells her, smoothing her hair with her wet hands, just like Dancy's doing. "I don't even think you're going to have to worry about Waycross, or Sinethella and her hound, or the nine crazy ladies in their big house in Savannah, not the way things are going."

"I don't even know what you're talking about. Who's Sinethella?"

The mirror girl looks skeptical and furrows her brow. "It hasn't even told you about—"

"He tells me what I need to know, when I need to know it. He tells me—"

"Just enough to keep you moving, and not one word more, because it knows the big picture would shut you down, send you running off back to the swamp with your tail tucked between your legs."

"I don't have a tail," Dancy says, wishing the albino girl in the mirror, the girl who isn't her reflection after all, would shut up and go away.

"You might as well, as far as the seraphim are concerned. To them, you're nothing but a trained monkey, an ugly little freak of evolution they can swindle into wiping their heavenly asses for them."

"Is this another test?" Dancy asks the mirror, and she imagines balling up her fist and punching the glass as hard as she can, imagines the blood and pain, the glittering shards and the silvery sound they would make falling into the rust-stained sink.

"Christ, you can be a tiresome little cunt," the girl in the mirror sighs, and now her face is changing, years rolling through her rose-colored eyes like waves against a sandy shore, waves to diminish her grain by grain and draw deep lines in her pale skin. And, in only a moment more, the girl in the mirror is a grown woman—thirty, thirty-five, forty—looking backwards at the lost child she was, or Dancy's only looking ahead to the lost woman she'll become, if she lives that long. *Or maybe it works both ways*, Dancy thinks, and she reaches out, expecting their fingers to brush, but there's only the cold, impenetrable surface of the looking glass and her own sixteen-year-old face gazing back at her again.

"Just a trick," Dancy whispers, even though she doesn't really believe it. "The angel said there would be lots of tricks."

The girl in the mirror says nothing more or less than Dancy says, and does nothing that she doesn't do, and Dancy Flammarion turns her back on the sink, and whatever it might, or might not, mean. She makes sure her jeans are zipped, and tightens her belt again, and unlocks the restroom door.

Dancy's holding a red-and-white can of Campbell's Chicken & Stars soup, the label enough to make her mouth water, and she thinks briefly about trying to steal it before she sets it back on the shelf. She glances towards the screen door leading out to the cloudy day and the old man and the front of the Texaco station. There's a shiny black pickup truck idling by the pumps, and the old man is talking to the driver. No one who's looking for her, just someone who's stopped to buy gas or a pack of cigarettes, someone the old man knows, or maybe he talks like that to everyone who stops. Maybe he offers everyone a wintergreen Certs and tells them to be sure and flush.

"He's a son of a bitch," she hears the old man say. "When the Good Lord was handin' out assholes, that cocksucker went back for seconds."

The driver of the black truck laughs, laughs the way that fat men and very small demons laugh, and Dancy looks at the can of soup again.

"Son of a whore wanted his money back," the old man says. "I told him sure thing, just as soon as ol' Gabriel starts playin' taps."

The man from the black truck laughs again, and Dancy's empty stomach rumbles.

And then she looks the other way, towards the rear of the store. There's another screen door back there that she didn't notice before she went into the restroom, a door with a wooden plaque hung above it, but she has to get closer to read all the words painted on it. *Hyenas will howl in their fortified towers And jackals in their luxurious palaces,* the plaque declares in fancy calligraphied letters like the ones on the cover of her grandmother's old Bible. *Her fateful time also will soon come And her days will not be prolonged. Isaiah 13:19–22.*

"I'm doing my part," she whispers, reaching for the brass door handle, smelling the musky wild-animal smell getting in through the screen wire. "Now you better keep him busy long enough for me to finish this, you hear?"

The angel doesn't answer her, but then it rarely ever does, so she doesn't take the silence one way or another.

The door creaks very loudly, like the hinges have never once seen so much as a single drop of oil, the hinges and the long spring that's there to snap the door closed again. Dancy steps over the threshold, eases the noisy door shut behind her, and now she's standing on a small back porch cluttered with an assortment of crates and cardboard boxes and greasy, rusting pieces of machinery that she doesn't recognize.

And before she even sees the cage, before she sees what's waiting *in* the cage, Dancy Flammarion is out on the highway again, the air filled with that thunder that isn't thunder, and the seraph shrieks and slices the storm-damp air with its sword of fire and molten steel.

The scorching light pouring from the angel's purple-blue eyes almost blinds her, and she turns her head away.

In His right hand He held seven stars, and out of His mouth came a sharp double-edged sword. His face was like the sun shining in all its brilliance—

On the porch behind the Texaco station, Dancy reaches for her knife, the big carving knife she used in Bainbridge, something else salvaged from the cabin in Shrove Wood. But her knife is still tucked safely inside the duffel bag, and her bag's out front with the old man.

And then she sees the cage, big enough to hold at least five panthers, a great confining box of thick steel bars and seam welds and black iron bolts. But the only thing inside is a naked woman huddled in the dirt and filthy hay covering the floor of the cage. Her long auburn hair hangs about her narrow face in knots and matted coils, and her skin is so streaked with shit and mud and grime that Dancy can't be sure if she's black or white or some other color altogether. The woman looks up, her eyes so deep and dark and filled with pain, and when she speaks Dancy thinks that it's surely the most broken and desperate voice she's ever heard from simple human lips.

"Help me," the woman pleads. "You *have* to help me. He's insane."

Dancy slowly descends the four steps to the weathered square of concrete laid between the porch and the cage, and stands only five or six feet back from the bars. "That old man locked you up in there?" she asks, and there are tears streaming from the woman's brown eyes, eyes the same rich brown as chocolate. She nods her head and reaches through the bars for Dancy.

I don't have my knife, she thinks, half praying to anything that's listening, and Dancy imagines the angel's fiery sword sweeping down to divide her careless soul from her flesh, to burn her so completely that there'll be nothing left to send to Hell.

"He's crazy," the woman says. "He's going to *kill* me. Whoever you are, you *have* to help me."

"He said there was a live panther back here," Dancy tells her and looks over her shoulder at the back door of the little store, wondering if the old man is still busy talking to the guy in the pickup truck about the cocksucker who went back for seconds.

"I just told you. He's insane. He'll say anything. *Please—*"

"He put you in that cage? Why'd he do that? Why didn't he just kill you?"

"You're not *listening* to me!" the woman hisses and bares her teeth; her voice has changed, has grown as angry and impatient as it was desperate and broken only a few seconds before. "We don't have much *time*. He'll figure out you're back here and come after you."

Dancy looks at the heavy Yale padlock holding the cage door shut, and then she looks back at the woman. "I don't have the key," she says. "How am I supposed to open that, if I don't have the key?"

The woman's dark eyes glimmer and flash, and Dancy realizes that they're not the same color they were before, the deep and chocolate brown replaced suddenly by amber shot through with gleaming splinters of red. She retreats one step, then another, putting that much more distance between herself and the naked woman in the cage.

"I *know* who you are, Dancy Flammarion. I know what you did in Bainbridge. I know about the angel." And the woman's voice has changed again, too. This is the voice of an animal that has learned to talk, or a human being who's forgetting. "I know you've been sent here to save me."

"Who told you that?" Dancy asks, and she kicks at a loose bit of concrete, pretending that she isn't afraid. "I was just looking for the panther, that's all."

"We don't have *time* for this shit," the woman growls and seizes the iron bars in both hands, and now Dancy can see the long black claws where her fingernails used to be. The naked woman, who isn't really a woman at all, slams herself against the bars so hard that the whole cage shakes and the padlock rattles loudly.

"Now open this fucking cage!"

"Don't you talk to me like that," Dancy says; her face feels hot and flushed, and her heart's beating so fast she thinks maybe it

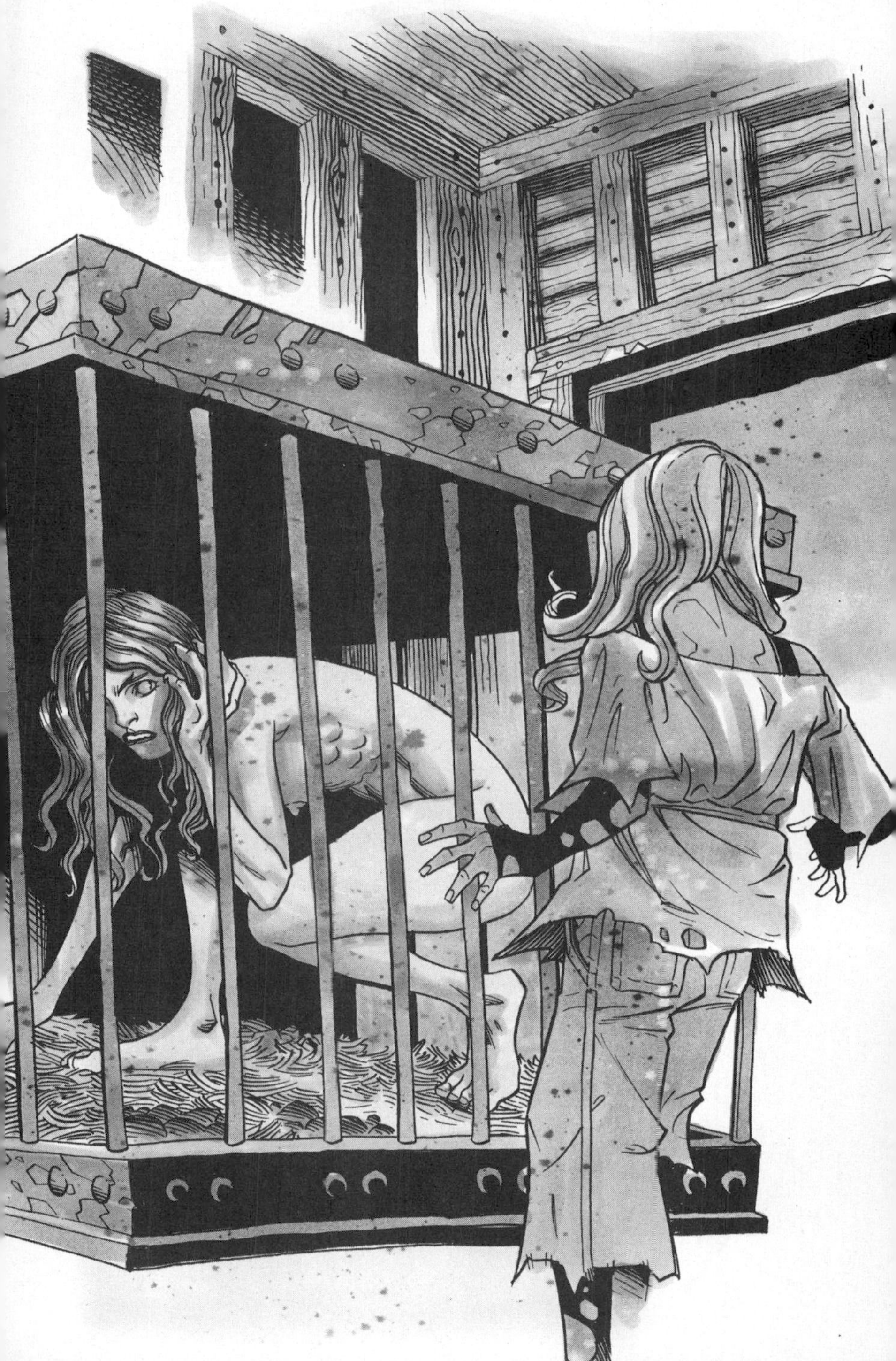

means to explode. "I don't care what you are. I don't like to be talked to that way."

The thing in the cage presses its face to the bars, and its thick lips curl back to show Dancy eyeteeth that have grown long and sharp, the teeth of something that hunts for its supper, something that might even send a panther packing. Its amber eyes blaze and spark, and Dancy tries not to imagine the soul burning beneath its skin, inside that skull, a soul so hot it will wither her own if she doesn't look away.

"What? You think you're some kind of holy fucking *saint*," it snarls and then makes a sound that isn't precisely laughter. "Is that it? You think you're something so goddamn pure that strong language is gonna make your ears bleed?"

"I think maybe it's a good thing, you being in that cage," Dancy replies, almost whispering now.

And the thing locked in the iron cage roars, half the cheated, bottomless fury in the whole world bound up in that roar, and then it slams itself against the bars again. Its bones have begun to twist and pop, rearranging themselves inside its shifting skin. Its hands have become a big cat's paws, sickle talons sheathed in velvet, and its spine buckles and stretches and grows a long tail that ends in a tuft of black fur.

And Dancy turns to run, because she doesn't have her knife, because somehow she wasn't ready for this, no matter what she saw in Bainbridge or Shrove Wood, no matter if maybe those things were more terrible; maybe the angel was wrong about this one. She turns to run, running for the first time, and she'll worry about the angel later, but the old man is right there to stop her. He holds her firmly by the shoulders and grins down at her with his tobacco-stained teeth.

"Where you goin', sport? I thought you *wanted* to see my panther?"

"Let go of me. I told you I ain't got three dollars."

"Hey, that's right. You did say that. So that makes this sort of like stealin', don't it? That means you *owe* me somethin'," and he spins her roughly around so she's facing the cage again. The thing inside has changed so much that there's hardly any trace of the cowering, filthy woman left; it paces restlessly, expectantly, from one side of the cage to the other, its burning, ravenous eyes never leaving Dancy for very long. And she can still hear its animal voice inside her head.

You were supposed to save me, it lies. *You were supposed to set me free.*

"Big ol' cat like that one there," the old man says and spits a stream of Beech-Nut onto the concrete, "she'll just about eat a fella out of house and home. And seein' as how you owe me that three bucks—"

"Do you even know what you've got in that cage, old man? You got any idea?"

"Near enough to know she ain't none too picky in her eatin' habits."

"You don't hold a thing like that with steel and locks," Dancy says, matching the monster's gaze because she knows this has gone so far that it'll be worse for her if she looks away.

"Oh, don't you fret about locks. I might not be old Mr. Merlin at the goddamn round table, but I can cast a binding good enough. Now, tell me somethin', Dancy," the old man says and shoves her nearer the cage. "How far'd you think you'd get after that mess you made down in Bainbridge? You think they were gonna just let you stroll away, pretty as you please?"

And she reaches for her grandfather's straight razor, tucked into the back pocket of her jeans, not her knife but it's plenty enough to deal with this old wizard.

"You think there's not gonna be a price to pay?" he asks, watching the thing in the cage, and he doesn't even notice until it's too late, and she's folded the razor open. The blade catches the dull, cloud-filtered sun and shines it back at her.

"Whole lot of good folks out there want you dead, sport. Lots of folks, they want you fuckin' *crucified*. It's only a matter of time before some ol' boy puts you down for what you done."

But then she slips free of his big, callused hands, and before the old man can say another word, she's slashed him twice across the face, laying open his wrinkled forehead all the way to the bone and slicing a three-inch gash beneath his chin that just misses his carotid artery. The old man yelps in pain and surprise and grabs for her, but Dancy steps quickly to one side and shoves him stumbling towards the cage. He trips and goes down hard on his knees; the wet crunch of shattered bone is loud, and the thing that isn't a woman or a panther stops pacing and lunges towards the bars and the old man.

"Yeah, that may be so," Dancy says, breathless, blood spattered across her face and T-shirt and dripping from the razor to the cracked gray concrete. "But *you* won't be the one to do it."

And then the thing is on him, dragging the old man up against the side of the cage, its sickle claws to part his clothes and flesh like a warm fork passing through butter, but he only screams until it wriggles its short muzzle between the bars and bites through the top of his skull. The old man's body shudders once and is still. And then the thing looks up at her, more blood spilling from its jaws, flecks of brain and gore caught in its long whiskers.

"Well?" it growls at her. "You gonna do what they sent you here to do, or you just gonna stand there all damn day with your mouth hanging open?"

Dancy nods her head once, wanting to tell it that there's no way she could have ever opened the cage door, even if she had the key, even if the angel hadn't told her to kill them both.

"Then you best stop gawking and get to work."

And Dancy wipes the bloody razor on her jeans, then folds it shut, and she runs back up the steps to the cluttered porch and the noisy screen door and the shadows waiting for her inside the little store.

It doesn't take her very long to find what she's looking for among the dusty shelves and pegboard wall displays, a cardboard box of Diamond kitchen matches and a one-gallon gasoline can. She takes out a handful of the wooden matches and puts them in her pocket, tears away the strip of sandpaper on the side of the box, and puts that in her pocket, as well. Then Dancy gets a paper bag from behind the cash register and also takes some of the Campbell's Chicken & Stars soup and a handful of Zero bars, some Slim Jims, and a cold bottle of Coca-Cola. While she's bagging the food, she hears thunder, and at first she thinks that it's the angel, the angel come back around to check up on her, to be sure she's doing it right. But then there's lightning and the *tat-tat-tat* of rain starting to fall on the tin roof, so she knows it's only another thunderstorm. She rolls the top of the paper bag down tight and tells herself it's not stealing, not really, that she's not taking much and nothing that she doesn't need, so whatever it is, it isn't stealing.

Over the staccato patter of the rain against the roof, she can hear the noises the cat thing in its cage is making as it tears the old man apart. She thinks about looking for a key to the cage, no matter what the angel has said. The old man might have it hidden in the register, or somewhere in the clutter behind the counter, or in an old snuff tin somewhere. She might get lucky and find it, if it's even there to be found, if she spends the rest of the afternoon searching the Texaco station. Or she might not. And anyway, there would still be the binding spell, and she wouldn't know where to begin with that.

"It's just another monster," Dancy says, as though saying the words aloud might make it easier for her to believe them. And she remembers her mother reading to her from the Bible about King Darius and Daniel and the angel God sent down to shut the mouths of the lions in the pit. Would it even be grateful, the thing in the cage, or would it try to kill her for setting it free? And would her angel shut its mouth, or would it let the thing eat her the way it's eating the old man? Would that be her punishment for disobeying the angel's instructions?

Then there's another thunderclap, louder than the first, loud enough to rattle the windows, and this time the lightning follows almost right on top of it, no seconds in between to be counted, no distance to calculate, and Dancy takes her brown paper bag and the matches and the gas can and goes out to the pumps. The screen door slams shut behind her, and she finds her duffel bag right where she left it with the old man, beneath the corrugated tin awning. The rain's not coming down so hard as she thought, but she has a feeling it's just getting started. She opens the duffel and tucks the paper bag inside with her clothes and the carving knife, then Dancy shoulders the heavy duffel again and steps out from beneath the cover of the awning.

The rain feels good, the soothing tears of Heaven to wash her clean again, and she goes to the pump marked REGULAR, switches it on, and fills the gasoline can to overflowing. Then she lays the nozzle down on the ground at her feet, and the fuel gushes eagerly out across the gravel and the mud and cement. Dancy takes a few steps back, then stands there in the rain and watches the wide puddle that quickly forms around the pumps. She wrinkles her nose at the fumes, and glances up at the low purple-black clouds sailing past overhead. The rain speckles her upturned face; it's cold, but not unpleasantly so.

"Is this really what you want from me?" she asks the clouds, whatever might be up there staring down at her. "Is this really what happens next?" There's no answer, because the angel doesn't ever repeat itself.

Dancy picks up the gas can, and there's a moment when she's afraid that it might be too heavy now, that the weight of the

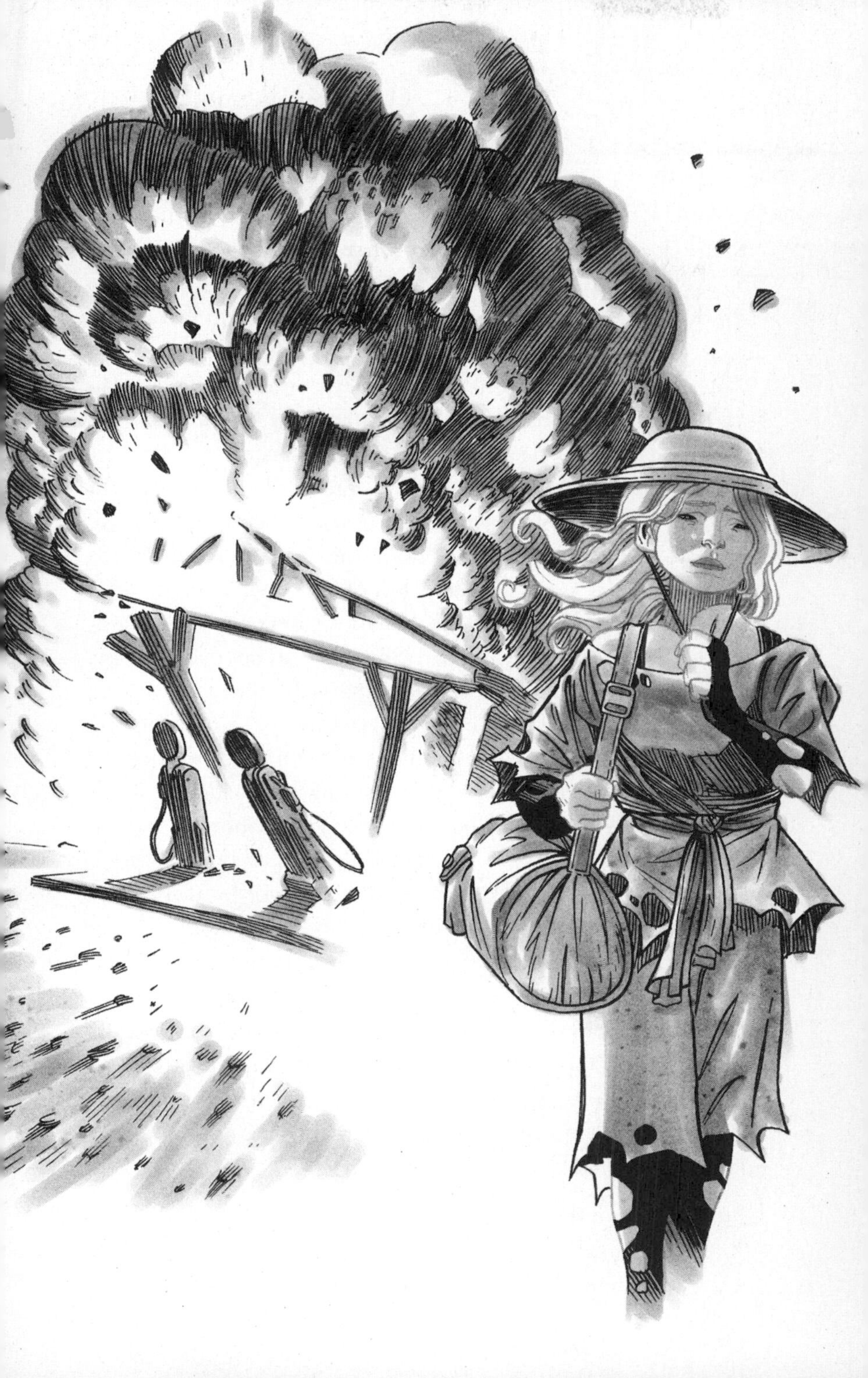

duffel bag and the full can together might be too much for her to manage. But then she shifts the duffel to one side, ignoring the pain as the thick canvas strap cuts into her right shoulder, and the can doesn't seem so heavy after all. She splashes a stream of gasoline that leads from the pumps, across the highway and then down the road for another hundred yards, before she stops and sets down the almost empty can.

This is what I do, she thinks, taking one of the matches and the rough strip of cardboard from her pocket. *Just like our cabin, just like that old church in Bainbridge, this is what I do next.*

She strikes the match and drops it onto the blacktop, and the gasoline catches fire immediately, a yellow-orange beast, undaunted by the summer rain, blooming to life to race hungrily back the way she's come. Dancy gets off the highway as quickly as she can and crouches low in a shallow, bramble- and trash-filled ditch at the side of the road. She squeezes her eyes shut and covers her ears, trying not to think about the thing in the iron cage, or the naked woman it pretended to be, or the old man who would have fed her to the monster, trying not to think of anything but the angel and all the promises it's made.

That there will someday be an end to this, the horrors and the blood, the doubt and pain, the cleansing fires and the killing.

That she is strong, and one day soon she will be in Paradise with her grandmother and grandfather and her mother, and even though they will know all the terrible things she's had to do for the angel, they'll still love her, anyway.

And then she feels the sudden rush of air pushed out before the blast, and Dancy makes herself as small as she can, curling fetal into the grass and prickling blackberries, and the ancient, unfeeling earth, indifferent to the affairs of men and monsters, gods and angels, trembles beneath her.

Bainbridge

I. Dry Creek Road

Only a few miles south and west of the sleeping city of electric lights and sensible paved streets, where a crooked red-clay road ends finally before nettle thickets and impassable cypress swamps leading away through the night to the twisting, marshy banks of the Flint River, sits the ruined husk of Grace Ebeneezer Baptist Church. Erected sometime late in 1889 by two freed slaves from Alabama, forsaken now by any Christian congregation for more than two decades, it has become another sort of sanctuary. Four straight white walls, no longer precisely white nor standing precisely straight, rise from a crumbling foundation of Ocala Limestone to brace the sagging gray roof, most of its tar-paper shingles lost over the years to summer gales and autumn storms. In places, the roof has collapsed entirely, open wounds to expose decaying pine struts and ridge beams, to let in the rain and falling leaves and the birds and squirrels that have built their nests in the rafters. Here and there, the holes go straight on through the attic floor, and on nights when the moon is bright, clean white shafts fall on the old pews and rotting hymnals. But this night there is no moon. This night there are only low black clouds and heat lightning, a persistent, distant rumble somewhere to the north of Dry Creek Road, and Dancy Flammarion stands alone on the cinder-block steps leading up to the wide front doors of the church.

There are two dozen or more symbols drawn on the weathered doors in what looks like colored chalk and charcoal. She recognizes some of them, the ones that the angel has warned her about or that Dancy learned from her grandmother before she died—an Egyptian eye of Horus and something that looks like a letter *H* but she knows is really the rune Hagal, a pentagram, an open, watchful eye drawn inside a triangle, a circle with a fish at its center. They're all there for the same reason, to keep her out, to keep whatever's hiding inside safe, as if *she* were the monster.

As if she's the one the angel wants dead.

Dancy's dreamed of this place many times, a hundred nightmares spent on this old church brooding alone at the nub end of its narrow, muddy road, the steeple that lists a bit to one side, threatening to topple over, the tiny graveyard almost lost to blackberry briars and buckeye, ferns and pokeweed. At *least* a hundred times, a hundred dream-sweat nights, she's walked the long path to this place, and sometimes the doors have no protective symbols to ward her off, but are standing open, waiting for her, inviting her to enter. Sometimes, the stained-glass windows and the empty window frames where all the glass has been broken out are filled with flickering orange light, like dozens of candles or maybe light from a bonfire someone's built inside the church. Tonight, the windows are dark, even darker than the summer sky.

She sets her heavy duffel bag down on the cinder blocks, which were painted green a very long time ago. Now, though, most of the green paint has flaked away or is hidden beneath a thick crust of moss and lichens. Dancy opens the canvas bag, and it only takes her a moment to find what she's looking for, the big carving knife she's carried all the way from Florida and the burned-out cabin on Eleanore Road. She ties the duffel bag closed again, and looks up at the sky just as a silent flash of lightning illuminates the clouds and silhouettes the craggy limbs of the trees pressing in close around the churchyard.

"Please," she says, "if there's another way," and from the other side of the door there are sounds like small claws against the dry wood and a woman's nervous laughter, and Dancy squeezes her eyes shut.

"I *don't* have to do this," she says, trying to ignore the noises coming from the church. "There *must* be somebody else besides me, somebody stronger or older or more—"

Something slams itself hard against the inside of the door, and Dancy screams as the carving knife slips from her sweaty fingers—

—and the church doors splinter and burst open, unleashing a gout of freezing, oily blackness that flows down the cinder-block steps towards her. Darkness that's not merely the absence of light, but a darkness so absolute that only in passing has it even dared to imagine the *possibility* of light, darkness become a living force possessed of intellect and hate, memory and appetite. It surges greedily around Dancy's legs, stickier than roofing pitch, tighter than steel jaws about her calves, and in a moment more it has begun to drag her towards the open doorway—

—and Dancy catches the knife in the last second before it strikes the cinder-block steps, and she shakes off the deception, nothing but some unguarded scrap of childhood fear turned against her. She glances over her left shoulder, wondering if the angel's hiding itself somewhere in the trees, if it's watching just in case she needs help.

You never needed anyone's help before, her dead mother whispers. *That night at the creek, the night it dragged me down to the deep place, or that day in the wood, you didn't need anyone's help with the first two.*

"With those first two, I had the shotgun," Dancy tells her, which is the truth, and she wishes that she'd thought to take her grandfather's Winchester out of the cabin in Shrove Wood before she burned it to the ground.

It wasn't the shotgun killed them, her mother whispers, her voice like someone that's trying to drown and talk at the same time.

"It helped, I reckon," Dancy says. "It was better than having nothing but this old knife. I don't know if you've noticed, but it's not even very sharp anymore."

This time her mother doesn't bother to answer, so Dancy knows that she's alone again, no murdered ghosts and no vengeful angels, and so it's time; she takes a deep breath and stares at the doors to the old church, the peeling white paint and the symbols that have been put there to keep her out. Then Dancy uses the tip of the knife to cut something invisible into the air, something like the sign of the cross, only there are more lines and angles to it. She does it exactly the way the angel said to, her own secret magic to undo all the monsters' hexes, and then the albino girl climbs the last two steps and reaches for one of the rusted iron door handles. She isn't surprised that the door isn't locked.

II. *Pensacola Beach (December 1982)*

Julia Flammarion sits alone in the dingy motel room across the street from the Gulf of Mexico, watching the brilliant winter sun outside the wide windows. There are seagulls like white Xs drawn on the sky. The room smells like disinfectant and the menthol cigarettes the man she slept with the night before was smoking. His name was Leet—Andrew Leet—unless he was lying and his name was really something else. He got angry when she asked him to use a rubber, and he called her a skinny redneck bitch and said he ought to call the police because he knew she wasn't really eighteen, but then he used one, anyway. He was gone when she woke up, and there was twenty-five dollars and thirty-three cents lying on top of the television. She's holding all the money in her left hand, crumpled into a tight wad. Her mother would say this means she's a whore now, even though she didn't ask Andrew Leet for the money and she knows that he only left it to get even with her for making him use a rubber.

The television's on, because she doesn't like the silence, doesn't want to be alone in the motel room with nothing but the sound of her own thoughts and the wind and squawking seagulls and the traffic out on Ariola Drive. She turned the volume up loud and left it on a channel that was nothing but news and weather, all day and all night long. Back home, there's no television, and not much of anything else, either.

Julia thinks that maybe she'll use some of the money to buy breakfast at the IHOP a little farther down the strip. She's always wanted to eat breakfast at an IHOP, blueberry pancakes and link sausages and black coffee and orange juice; besides, it isn't enough money for another night in the motel. Not that she needs another night. She's been in Pensacola Beach almost a whole week, a week since the bus ride from Milligan, and she's done almost everything that she came here to do. She's had sex with four men. She's seen two movies in a real theater, *Sophie's Choice* and *Gandhi*. She's gotten drunk on frozen strawberry daiquiris, learned to smoke, and she's watched the moon rise and the sun set over the ocean. She bought a yellow Minnie Mouse T-shirt at a souvenir shop and wore it so people might think she'd had enough money to go all the way to Disney World. She hitchhiked back across the three-mile-long Pensacola Bay Bridge and all the way to the zoo in Gulf Breeze, where she saw more kinds of animals and birds and snakes than she'd ever really believed existed. She'd bought a red bikini and then spent hours walking up and down the beach, where she found cockles and periwinkle shells and two shark's teeth. She got a sunburn and watched teenagers skateboarding. She'd met a drunk old woman outside a bar who told her stories about hurricanes and her lazy ex-husband who'd turned out to be a homosexual.

Behind her, the angel makes an angry sound like a forest fire, like she's back home and all Shrove Wood is going up in smoke, but Julia keeps her eyes on the pale blue sky and the hungry, wheeling gulls.

"It don't make no difference to me," she tells the angel. She knows it isn't real, that it's only something wrong with her head makes her hear and see angels and worse things than angels, but she also knows it's usually easier if she doesn't ignore them when they speak to her. "You do as you please. I've come this far. I'm not going to chicken out now."

The room fills with a smell like hot asphalt and fresh lemons, but she doesn't look away from the window.

"You're just gonna have to find another crazy girl," Julia tells the angel. " 'Cause this one's done with you. You can fly right the fuck back to Heaven or St. Peter or whoever it is you came from and tell them I said to mind their own damn business from here on out."

There's a sudden crackling noise from the television, and Julia almost turns to see.

"You go and break that, I can't afford to pay for it," she says. "Leave me alone."

The angel clacks its teeth together, *clack, clack, clack*, and the hot asphalt and lemon smell gets worse.

"No," Julia says and reaches for the remote control to turn off the television so that maybe it'll stop making the static sound. She presses OFF, but nothing happens. "Fuck you," she says, and the angel hisses. She prayed that it wouldn't follow her, that maybe it would get lost or distracted somewhere between Milligan and Pensacola, but it didn't. Every single thing she's done the last six days, its been right there behind her. It watched her while she fucked Andrew Leet and those other men. It wandered the theater aisle while she watched *Gandhi* and *Sophie's Choice*. It floated above the reptile house at the zoo.

"You ain't been listening to me, but you should. I said you can't have me, and soon enough you'll see that I *mean* what I'm saying."

The angel screams, and its wings are thunderclaps and St. Elmo's fire trapped there inside the motel room with Julia. But it knows she's not afraid of it anymore, and she *knows* that it knows. Before she took all the money her mother kept hidden in a Mason jar under the front porch and left the wood for good, Julia went out to the sandy place where she'd seen the angel the very first time. That was seven years ago, when she was still just a little girl. A wide clearing in the slash pine and briars and Spanish bayonets, and sometimes rattlesnakes and copperheads sunned themselves there. The first time she'd seen the angel, there'd been a huge canebrake rattler stretched out on the hot sand, and the angel had burned it until there was nothing left but charcoal. Before she took the money and set out for Milligan, she went back to the clearing and called the angel and told it that it couldn't have her. She wasn't going to be some sort of saint or nun or something, and she wasn't going to end up like crazy old Miss Sue Anne who lived by herself in a shack on the far side of the deep lake at the end of Wampee Creek. There were crumbling plaster statues stuck up all around the shack, statues of the Virgin Mary and Jesus and St. Giles, the patron saint of people who are afraid of the night. And sometimes Miss Sue Anne rowed out onto the lake in a leaky boat and said prayers and did root magic so all the evil things God had told her lived in the mud at the bottom couldn't come up to the surface.

"What I said, I still mean every goddamn word of it," Julia says, having to raise her voice to be heard above the television and the racket that the angel's making. "You go find someone else, someone who *wants* whatever it is you're selling, 'cause you can't have me."

And then the angel tells her what happens to suicides, tells her for the hundredth time all about the special corner of Hell reserved for people who are that cowardly, people who think they know better than God when and where and how they ought to die. And when it's finally finished, the angel slips away, taking all the noise and the strange smells with it. And Julia sits on the edge of the bed, biting her lip so she won't start crying, and she tries hard to think about nothing but blueberry pancakes.

III. Pensacola Beach (December 1982)

When Julia Flammarion has finished her late breakfast—the stack of blueberry pancakes with blueberry syrup and butter and a little dollop of whipped cream on top—she leaves a ten-dollar tip for her waitress and then pays the woman at the register. The cashier tells Julia to have a nice day and come again, and Julia smiles for her and thinks perhaps this is the very last person who will ever see her smile. She leaves the IHOP and walks west on Ariola, back towards the dingy motel room that is no longer hers. She has six dollars and some change remaining from the money that Andrew Leet left on the television. Her whore money. Julia leaves the sidewalk and wanders out between the sea oats and the low white dunes onto the beach. The sun is warm, even though the wind is colder than it was the day before. She pulls the lime-green cardigan tighter about her shoulders and buttons it. It's one of the few things she took with her from the cabin in Shrove Wood. Her mother gave it to her as a birthday present two years ago; there are small pink flowers around the cuffs and the collar, and she didn't want to leave it behind.

Past the motel, Julia comes upon a man sitting on a produce crate in the sand, picking a twelve-string guitar, playing some song she's never heard before, so maybe it's something he wrote himself. She stands there listening, watching his fingers pulling the music from the strings, and when the song's finished, she puts the rest of the money in his open guitar case. He grins and thanks her, this shabby, handsome, easy man, the sort of man that would have made her daddy scowl, the sort he'd have probably called a no-account hippie freak. She wishes that at least one of the men who'd been her lovers over the last six days could have had this man's eyes or his strong, callused fingers or the soft light that seems to hang about his face. Her men were all ogres, she thinks, cursing and pawing at her, slobbering and grunting like hogs when they came. This man would have been different. He asks her name, and she tells him the truth, then thanks him and walks away as he begins playing another song she's never heard. She would have liked to stay and listen to it all and any other songs that he wanted to play for her, but hearing more of that music, she might have changed her mind.

Julia follows the beach, the sand that is so white it makes her doubt the beaches in Heaven could possibly be any whiter, the water like peacock feathers lapping at the shore, vivid green blue going hyacinth out where the sea starts getting deep. And there are no clouds in the sky today, and she thanks Jesus for there being a sky like that. She figures that he's still listening to her prayers, even if she is a thief and a whore. Mary Magdalene was a whore, too.

Julia finds a cinnamon-colored starfish, wider than her hand and half-buried in the sand, and stoops to look at it. But she doesn't touch it. The starfish might still be alive. *Leave it be*, she thinks. *Let me just look at it a moment more.* And she's still looking at it when she hears the angel somewhere close behind her, its wings scorching the day. The starfish begins to steam and writhe in the sand, five arms curling in upon themselves, and the cold gulf water hisses against it. In a moment, it has shriveled and gone as black as the rattlesnake did that morning in the clearing when she first met the angel.

"That wasn't necessary," she says. "Destroying beautiful things isn't going to change my mind," and the angel makes a spiteful, sizzling sound. Then it tells her the day and the hour that the handsome man with the guitar will die, and it reminds her, again, what happens to suicides.

With the toe of her left sneaker, Julia heaps wet sand over the scorched starfish so she won't have to look at it. But only a second or two later, the sea sweeps in and uncovers it again.

"Maybe if you were real," she says, "I might be more afraid of you." She looks up, staring out across the water. There's a yellow fishing boat floating in the distance, a canary speck against all the blue. She wishes it were summer and that the sea wasn't so cold.

For the hundredth time, the angel tells her that she's a sane woman, but Julia knows that's a lie.

"Even if it were true," she says, "you might just as easily be a demon as an angel. You sure seem a lot more like a demon to me. Even if you *were* real, I don't think I'd believe in you. That's still my choice, you know?"

Look at me, Julia, the angel says. *Turn and behold me. Look upon me and know that I am but one fraction of the innumerable host of the Ancient of Days.*

"Go away," Julia replies. "I don't want to listen to you anymore. You make me angry, and I don't want to be angry at the end."

The angel howls and hacks at the morning air with its four wings like hatchets of flame. The air around Julia grows uncomfortably warm and a patch of the sea in front of her has begun to boil violently.

"It's *still* my choice," she says again. "Now leave me alone. Go haunt someone else."

Waves rushing up the sand towards her are dappled with the corpses of tiny silver fish and a small crab that have been boiled alive.

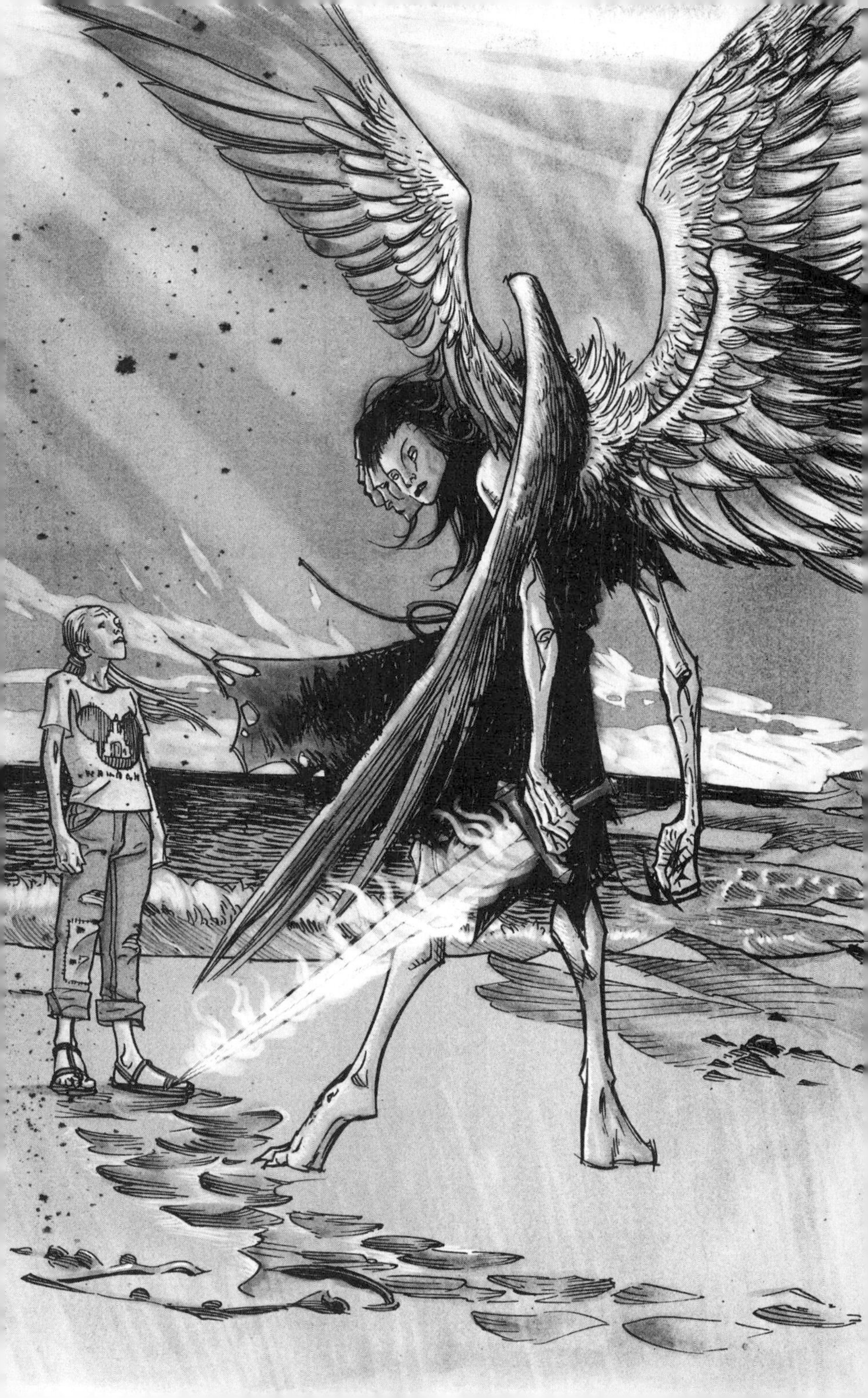

"It's still my choice," Julia says for the third time.

And then the angel is gone, and the sea has stopped bubbling. She waits a moment, then glances over her shoulder. Ten or fifteen feet behind her, there's a star-shaped place where the sand has been melted into a glassy crust. Back towards the motel, the man with the guitar is still sitting on his produce crate. He waves at her, and Julia waves back. And then she turns and wades into the surf, grateful now it's so cold that the waves breaking about her calves take her breath away. The sea has already swept the boiled fish farther down the beach. She shuts her eyes and recites the Lord's Prayer. She thinks of her mother and her father and the old cabin in Shrove Wood, and she thinks about the mostly wonderful week she's had in Pensacola Beach and Gulf Breeze, a whole lifetime in only six days, six days and a morning. She reminds herself it's more than a lot of people get, and when the water is as high as her waist, Julia opens her eyes and starts to swim.

IV. The Forsaken Church

After the unlocked doors and the things she saw coiled up in a corner of the foyer, things that might have been dead or might only have wanted her to think that they were dead, Dancy Flammarion stands between the rows of broken and upturned pews, already halfway down the aisle to the wrecked altar. She's surprised that there are so many of them hiding out in the old church, and wishes the angel might have been just a little more specific. They line the walls, black figures blacker than the summer night, shadows of shadows, and some of them have taken seats in the pews; several have slipped in behind her, blocking her way back to the doors. They have no faces, though a few of them might have eyes, brighter smudges of shadow set into their indistinct skulls. Some of them seem to have wings, and others move about on all fours like bobcats or coyotes made of spilled India ink, but most of them stand up straight and tall, as if they might fool her into thinking they were once men and women. They whisper expectantly among themselves, and here and there one of them sniggers nervously or grinds its teeth or taps its long claws against the back of a varnished pew.

"Will she kill us all?" one of them asks.

"What? With that silly little knife?" asks another.

"Perhaps we should choose a champion," another of the black figures suggests and several of them begin to laugh.

Dancy licks her lips, her mouth gone dry as dust, and she holds the carving knife out in front of her.

"Will you look at that, now," one of them cackles and takes a step towards her. "She's a regular white-trash Joan of Arc, wouldn't you say? Our Lady of Rags and Swamp Gas." And for a time, the old church fills up with the sound of their laughter. Dancy grips the wooden hilt of the knife and waits for whatever it is that she's supposed to do.

"We've been watching for you, child," one of the shades says. It's seated very near her, like the silhouette of something that's learned how to be a woman and a wolf at the same time. Its gray-smudge eyes flash a hungry emerald, and when it stands up, it's much, much taller than Dancy expected. "We've been hearing rumors about what happened down in Florida. There was a crow, wouldn't talk about nothing else. Miss Dancy Flammarion, the vengeful right hand of Jehovah, some pissed-off angel's albino concubine. But what the hell, you know? Rumors aren't usually much more than that, especially when you get them from crows. But here you stand, girl, big as life and twice as shabby," and the monsters laugh again.

"What I'm wondering," the wolf woman says, taking a step closer to Dancy, "is how you ever got yourself out of that insane asylum way down in Tallahassee. Or isn't that part of the rumors true?"

Dancy licks her lips again. "I can't fight you all," she says. "I wasn't sent here to fight you all."

More laughter, laughter loud enough to wake whatever dead might still lie sleeping in the overgrown cemetery next to Grace Ebeneezer Baptist Church. And the thing that is neither a wolf nor a woman, the thing that's hardly anything more than a patch of smoke and depravity and wishful thinking, cocks its head and blinks at her.

"Something else drew you here," Dancy tells it. "All of you. Something born of hurt and ill will, death and the cruelty of men, an old evil which lay a thousand years in the mud at the bottom of the river—"

"She's a regular William goddamn Shakespeare," the wolf-woman shade says, interrupting her, and there's more laughter from the black things that have taken refuge in the abandoned church. "We knew you were a force to be reckoned with, child, but no one mentioned you were a poet in the bargain."

"That's just what the angel told me," Dancy says, wishing she didn't sound so scared, wishing she'd known there'd be so many of them. "Something drew you here. And that's the one I've come for."

"I see," the shade replies and sits down in the pew again. "Fair enough, then. You won't have to wait much longer. She'll be along shortly, that one. In the meantime, why don't you have a seat here and—"

"You can't *trick* me," Dancy tells the shade and points her carving knife at it.

The others laugh again, but not quite as loudly as before. *Come and get me*, Dancy prays silently, because she knows the angel can hear her, wherever it's gone. *Please come now and take me away.*

"Why don't you kiss me," the thing on the pew purrs. "You'd be sweet, I bet. I wager you'd be just as sweet as spring water and strawberries. Me, I haven't had a kiss in such an awful long time. Has anyone *ever* kissed you, Dancy Flammarion? I mean, *besides* that angel of yours."

Dancy shifts the carving knife from one hand to the other and wipes her sweaty palm on the front of her T-shirt. The angel isn't coming for her. It led her here, and she followed of her own accord, and now it won't have anything else to do with her until she's finished what it's brought her here to do. The shade's eyes flash brilliant green again, and Dancy shakes her head and continues down the aisle towards the desecrated altar and the pulpit and the benches where a choir once sat on Sunday mornings when the sanctuary was filled with dazzling sunlight and song and a preacher's booming voice.

"Have it your way, kid," the wolf-woman shade calls out after her. "I'll just sit tight and watch the show. But if you change your mind, I'll be right here."

V. Pensacola Beach (December 1982)

Julia Flammarion swims until the cold has done its job, exactly what she's asked it to do for her, and her arms and legs have grown too stiff and numb to possibly swim any farther. Which means that she'll never be able to swim all the way back to shore, either, so there's no point losing her nerve now. It doesn't matter if she turns coward and changes her mind or decides that life as a crazy girl who talks to angels is still better than drowning in the Gulf of Mexico. She squints back towards the beach, nothing visible but a faint white stripe against the blue horizon, and wonders about the handsome man with the guitar, what he thought as she walked into the water in her clothes and shoes and began to swim away. Did he even notice? Is he watching her now? Has he gone looking for help? She hopes not. She hopes that he's still sitting there on his apple crate playing beautiful songs she'll never hear.

"And what now?" she asks the high and unconsoling sun, the sun that might as well be the eye of God staring bitterly down at a fifteen-year-old suicide. The eye of a God who's finally washing his hands of her once and for all. A moment later, Julia gets a big mouthful of saltwater, and it strangles her and burns her sinuses and throat.

"Is that your answer?" she sputters weakly, and the sun continues to hang mute in the cloudless winter sky, however many tens or hundreds of millions of miles away from her it might be.

Much too far to matter, she thinks, and shuts her eyes. The cold and the effort of swimming out this far have made her very sleepy, and so maybe *that's* what happens next. Maybe it's as simple as shutting her eyes and drifting on the swells until she falls asleep. Maybe there will even be one last dream, something warm and gentle that shows her another way her life might have gone, if she weren't insane and had never spoken to the angel that first day in the clearing in Shrove Wood. If the rattlesnake had never been burned to charcoal. If the angel had never started telling her stories about monsters. Julia uses the last of her strength to imagine a dream just like that, a very *good* dream in which she marries the handsome man with the guitar and they have children and even grandchildren and she grows old and dies at home in her bed with all of them about her. She tells herself that the sound of wings close by is nothing but a curious seagull or a pelican, and only a few seconds later, too exhausted to tread water any longer, she slips beneath the welcoming surface of the sea.

VI. The Demon of Hopekill Swamp

She might have had a name once, distant ages ago, before the white men came with their noisy, stinking cities and their clattering railroads and their murderous highways, back when the Muskogee were the only men she'd ever seen and who'd ever seen her. But if she *did* have a name, she's long since forgotten it. She might have had a mother, too, and perhaps even a father, like all the other things that creep and slither and swim and fly through the bayous and sloughs spread out along the Flint River. The shadow things hiding in the old church at the edge of the swamp call her Elandrion, Daughter of the Great Mother Nerpuz, but she's pretty sure it's just some shit they made up to stay on her good side and Elandrion wasn't ever really her name.

On this summer night, she's resting in the mud beneath a bald cypress log at the very bottom of a deep, still pool, gnawing the last pale shreds of flesh from the bones of a great bullhead catfish. The bullhead was a giant, seven feet from snout to tail, and maybe it lived at the bottom of the pool for twenty years or more before she crept up and wrapped it in her strong arms and cracked its skull open between her jaws. Nothing in this whole damn swamp that's even half a match for her, not the mud cats or the huge old snapping turtles, not the cottonmouth moccasins, not even the goddamned alligators. Nothing out here she can't make her dinner from, not if she's gone and set her sights on it.

She's using a claw to get at the last bits of the bullhead's brains when she hears the shadows calling out across the night to her, their voices tangling in Spanish moss and the limbs of the trees and dripping down into the black water.

Elandrion, she's finally come. She's here.

She's found us all, Elandrion. She's right here in the church.

For a moment, she considers ignoring them, leaving them to their own fates. She thinks about finishing with the catfish and then sleeping through the scorch of the coming day right here beneath this cypress log. Surely together they can handle one skinny human girl, even if there's any truth to the gossip she's heard from mockingbirds and egrets and a couple of red-winged blackbirds.

The albino girl. She's waiting here for you.

Deliver us, Elandrion.

Beneath the cypress log, she rolls her eyes and picks her teeth. She imagines the shadows doing their best to menace the girl, playing like they're the next worst thing under Heaven, and all the while they're whining into the night for deliverance. *Ought to leave the lot of them to whatever the kid's got in mind,* she thinks, but then she hears another voice oozing down through the stagnant water and the slime.

—an old evil which lay a thousand years in the mud at the bottom of the river—something drew you here—that's the one I've come for—

And under all the bluster, the girl child's so scared she's about to shit herself, but still . . .

How long since anyone or anything called *her* out?

How long since anything dared come *looking* for her?

And, besides, there's really no point denying that she relishes the way the shadow things in the old church simper and bow to her and offer up all their darkest, most laughable prayers. Once, they even lured a couple of teenagers into the church and then kept them there for her. When she was done with them, the shadows buried what was left in the overgrown cemetery. It'd be a shame if the rumors were true and the albino girl went and killed them all off.

She has a knife, one of the shadows whimpers.

Elandrion, she's something terrible. Something mad. There's angel fire in her eyes, Elandrion.

She squints into the silt and gloom at the bottom of the pool, considering that last part and recalling that one of the egrets said something about angels, something about purifying fire. But she hadn't given it a second thought. Egrets say all sorts of crazy things.

—something drew you here—that's the one I've come for—

She pushes the bullhead's stripped and needle-spined carcass aside and disturbs a fat, tasty-looking slider concealed inside a thicket of eelgrass. Any other time, she'd have snatched the turtle as it tried to slip away to find some other hiding place. But she hesitates, listening to the voices filling the Georgia night, and the slider escapes. But that's all right, she tells herself. The albino girl will fill up the empty nook in her belly that the turtle would have occupied, that nook and then some. It's been years since she last tasted human flesh, which is almost as sweet as the wild boar piglets she finds in the swamp, from time to time.

Will you squeal for me, sweet angel child? she thinks and grins there beneath the cypress log. *Will you squeal just like all the little pigs?*

And then she kicks off with her broad feet and rises slowly towards the shimmering surface.

She who has no name, not that she can recall, the one the cowering shadows in the church call Elandrion. The ancient she-thing that the black-brown men and the pink-white men out gigging frogs or checking their traps for muskrats and beaver have glimpsed, moving swiftly between the trees. They've called her lots of things—the demon of Hopekill Swamp, witch, haint, monster, freak, the gator woman. They have no end of names for her. At least the red-brown men knew better than to give her any name at all.

She squats in the water lilies and rushes at the edge of the pool, considering once more everything the birds have said, the careless chatter of warblers and blue jays. The air is still filled with the whispered calls of the cringing church shadows. And that *other* voice, which must be the girl's, frightened but bold, the voice of someone who believes things she's better off without. Then, the one whose name is not Elandrion gets to her feet and, moving quickly on her long legs, follows a deer trail out of the swamp and up to higher, drier ground, and every living beast and insect falls silent as she passes.

VII. The Dirty Work of Angels

The shadows gathered in the old church on Dry Creek Road have kept Dancy busy for the better part of an hour. Rushing her suddenly from behind, their not-quite insubstantial fingers tearing at her shabby clothes or snatching strands of her white hair, then darting away to safety again. They've taunted and jeered and mocked, hurled threats and mildewed hymnals, and they've promised her, again and again, that she won't live to see another sunrise. There are scratches on her arms and face, the best they can manage with their shadow claws and teeth, a few drops of blood to whet their appetites for what's to come. They've backed Dancy all the way down the narrow aisle to the pulpit, where she stands with her back to the altar, her carving knife held out and glinting faintly by the unsteady glow of their will-o'-the-wisp eyes. She's noticed that their eyes have gotten a lot brighter, as if tormenting her has stoked some furnace hidden within them.

"Would you run, child, if you could?" the wolf-woman shade asks Dancy, and then, addressing all the others—"Brothers and sisters, if we took pity on this poor, misguided ragamuffin and let her leave now, would she even have the good sense to go, before Elandrion gets here?"

For an answer, there are ugly gales of laughter, hoots and whoops and uproarious fits of giggling.

"Do what you like," Dancy tells them. "I'm not going anywhere until I've done what I came here to do." But this only makes the shadows laugh that much louder.

"Oh, little girl," the wolf-woman shade snorts, "you're so preciously earnest. Such a stalwart little urchin, you are. It's a crying shame there's just the one of you. A pity you won't last longer. If only we could bottle you, I daresay none of us would ever go hungry again."

And then Dancy hears something behind her, and she looks over her right shoulder to see the monster glaring down at her from the pulpit. Its gnarled fingers grip the edges of the lectern, fingers that end in sickle talons, and they sink into the rotten wood as though it were clay.

"You're Elandrion?" Dancy asks it, turning to face the monster, and it grins and stands up straighter, though its bandy hind legs and thorny, crooked spine hardly seem suited to standing upright at all. It's so tall that its head almost scrapes against the sagging sheetrock a good ten or twelve feet above her.

"That's not my name," the monster replies. "I let *them* call me that, but *you*, you should know better than to believe I have a name." And Dancy thinks the monster's rheumy mud and black-water voice must be the very soul of the swamp, this swamp and every other swamp and bog, every single marsh and slough that has ever been since the first morning of Creation, the creeping, impenetrable spirit of every quagmire and bayou and bottomless, tannin-stained lake. Since the days of dinosaurs and screeching pterodactyls and dragonflies big as herons, this thing must have lain waiting for her in the wet places of the world, biding its time, murmuring her name in its sleep.

It's too much for me, she thinks, but Dancy knows her angel believes otherwise and has no intention of coming for her until the monster's dead.

"Am I?" it asks, feigning disappointment, and the monster grins even wider than before. "But I've heard so many stories. All the birds know your name. The birds, they think you're the goddamn Second Coming or something. Yeah, they tweet and twitter and squawk your name just like you're the bloody Virgin Mary her own damn self, come down from Paradise to put matters right."

Dancy backs slowly away from the thing behind the pulpit, sparing a quick glance at the shadows. They've all fallen silent now, but have moved in closer to her. They loom up around her, stretching themselves tall and thin, made bolder by the monster's words, by the sight and stench and sound of it.

"No, you're something special," the monster says, and its wide, unblinking eyes remind Dancy of hardboiled eggs—no pupils or irises in there, just those two bulging white balls poking out below its scaly brow. They loll lifelessly from one side to the other as it speaks and leak viscous rivulets into the hair sprouting from its gaunt cheeks.

"I remember one like you, long time ago, five hundred fucking years if it's a day. A Miccosukee boy, but I don't recollect what they called him. He came looking for me, too. Thought he was toiling for the gods, just like you. I still got a few of his teeth stuck up under a rock somewhere."

"I didn't walk all the way out here just to listen to you talk," Dancy says, gripping the knife as tightly as she can and wishing again that it were her grandfather's Winchester shotgun, instead. The monster stops grinning and hunches down so the end of its flat nose is only inches from Dancy's face.

"No, I reckon not," it snarls, and she can feel its voice rattling about inside her chest. Dancy thinks it's probably some sort of miracle her heart's still beating after the force of those four words inside her.

"You come here to lay me low," the monster says, "to show me what for and make the night safe for decent folks, ain't that about right."

"Something like that," Dancy tells the monster the shadows call Elandrion, the thing her angel had no name for. It flares its nostrils and sniffs the air around her.

"Then I guess we'd best get to it," the monster sighs and stands up again. "I got other business this night besides killing you."

All the shadow things suddenly withdraw, pressing themselves flat against the crumbling walls of the church or retreating into the foyer or the exposed rafters. And Dancy Flammarion stands her ground and waits for the monster to make the first move.

VIII. Pensacola Beach (December 1982)

Held fast in invisible currents, Julia Flammarion drifts away from Santa Rosa Island towards deeper water. She's almost weightless now, suspended here in the twilight realm between two worlds; above her, the clamorous lands of sunlight and seagulls, and far below her feet, the silent, lightless lands of cold abyssal solitude. There was a long and terrible few seconds of panic when she opened her mouth and the sea rushed past her teeth, forcing its way down her throat, flooding her lungs and stomach. Her head and chest seared with that alien, saltwater fire as her life streamed so easily from between her parted lips, racing back towards the shifting mirror surface, a dancing line of bubbles like the silvery bells of jellyfish. But then the panic passed, because the dead don't need to breathe, and the pain passed, too, and now there's the most perfect peace she's ever known. Dimly, Julia thinks she must be sinking, and more dimly still, she wonders if the angel was right after all and maybe the gloom below her is only the yawning entrance of the burning Catholic Hell that awaits all suicides. Not that she ever really doubted it, but it would be nice to learn that it was all bullshit, her mother's god and Jesus on his cross and the angels and all the rest. It would be nice to float a bit longer, neither quite here nor quite there, not dead and not alive, and then her consciousness pulling free at last and nothing to take its place but compassionate oblivion.

She would ask no more of Heaven than that.

Julia's eyes flutter open as something that might have been a fish darts quickly past her face.

So, she thinks, *at least I'm not alone.*

And she's hoping that the fish comes back, that there might even be more than just the one, when a point of blue-white light appears in the murk far below her. Hardly more than a flicker at first, but then the water around her grows suddenly warmer, buoying her upwards as it rises, and the flicker blossoms into a dazzling wheel, so wide she can hardly even see its edges, spinning counterclockwise in the deep.

And then the wheel of light is gone, just as abruptly as it came, but the sea about Julia no longer seems peaceful or merciful or kind. And even half-awake, half-awake at best, she knows without knowing *how* she knows that something has come out of the wheel. The same way she knew she wasn't alone that first day in the clearing in Shrove Wood, the same way she always knew whenever the angel was about to start talking to her. And the panic returns, much worse than before, because this isn't simply pain or death; this is something unseen rising up towards her, and if there were a patron saint of suicides she'd pray that the unseen thing is only a shark or a barracuda, some great eel or stingray or sawfish, only sharp teeth and snapping jaws to take her apart, to tear her limb from limb and be done with this slow death.

And then she must be *more* than half-asleep, because the sea has vanished, and Julia Flammarion is walking through the wood on a sunny autumn day, late afternoon, only an hour or so left until dusk, and the fallen leaves crunch beneath her shoes as she follows Wampee Creek towards the small waterfall and the crystal-clear pool that fills a wide sinkhole. When she was younger, she swam there on very hot days, swimming naked beneath the pines and wax myrtles, the air all around filled with the joyous, raucous calls of birds and frogs and insects. She stops beside a familiar tree, wondering if it's all been nothing more than a daydream, her stealing the money and running off to Pensacola, the men and the movies and the drunk old woman whose husband left her because he was gay, nothing but something she wished that she had the courage to do. Julia laughs and leans against the tree, laughing that her imagination could ever get away from her like that, laughing because she's relieved and feels silly and because it's good to laugh here in the fading October sun and the long, familiar shadows. She sits down and wipes her eyes, and that's when Julia notices the albino girl walking towards her up the creek, the legs of her baggy overalls rolled past the knees.

Somewhere nearby, a crow calls out hoarsely, and the girl looks up. Julia can see that her eyes are pink, and her hair as fine and pale as corn silk. The girl, who can't be more than five or six years old, is holding a fat bullfrog in one hand. She sees Julia, too, and she smiles and begins splashing through the creek towards her.

"Look, Momma," the girl says, holding up the bullfrog. "Have you ever in all your life seen one this big?"

Look, Momma . . .

And Julia knows perfectly damn well that the albino girl's only mistaken her for someone else, and in a few seconds more, when she comes closer, the child will realize her mistake. But then the girl stops, the creek flowing about her bare legs, and the bullfrog slips from her fingers and swims quickly away.

"Momma?" the girl asks, looking down at her empty hand and then back up at Julia.

I'm sorry, child, Julia starts to tell her, *but I ain't your momma. I ain't nobody's momma*, but then the girl turns and begins splashing away down the creek towards the sinkhole. Julia stands up, ashamed that she's frightened the kid, even if she's not sure why. She starts to call out to the albino girl, wants to tell her to be careful because the rocks are slick and it's not far to the falls and—

—there's only the caressing sea again, pressing in on every inch of her, the half-lit sea filling her, drowning her because she's asked it to, the agreeable, indifferent sea washing her away—a handful of mud, a pinch of salt, blood and a bit of sand, but there's nothing of her that won't dissolve or disperse. Only a passing moment's sadness that the autumn day by Wampee Creek was merely some smidgen of delirium coughed out by her dying mind, her life's last cruel trick, when it's only her and the sea and—

No. Her and the sea *and* just one *other* thing, whatever it was came slithering up out of the wheel of light before her dream of Shrove Wood and the albino girl. The thing that isn't a shark or a barracuda, that isn't anything that belongs here. Nothing she can see, but Julia feels it, like tendrils of scalding water twining themselves tightly about her legs, forcing her back up towards the surface. And then it's *inside* her, burning, prying her body and soul apart to find some slender crevice in between.

A pillar of fire dragging her to life again.

A child with white-rabbit eyes.

And still and always, the world buzzes on like angry bees. Let it come and go, appear and vanish, for what have we to lose?

Blood and thunder, fire and a madwoman with a knife.

Have you ever in all your life seen one this big?

The briefest flicker of blue-white light, a searchlight beacon hiding itself in her womb, where no one will ever think to look.

The body of woman is like a flash of lightning . . .

There are arms around Julia, then, the strong arms of a man hauling her up and out of the angry, cheated sea, the man's voice shouting for help, the voices of other men and the slosh of saltwater breaking against their bodies and the hull of a boat painted yellow as sunflowers and canary birds. And before Julia Flammarion blacks out, she sees the boat's name printed boldly across its bow—*Gulf Angel.*

IX. *The End of the Beginning*

Dancy sits on one of the old marble headstones in the overgrown cemetery and watches the church burn down. She didn't start the fire; she isn't exactly sure what started the fire, but she knows that it's probably for the best. *Fire will make the earth here pure again*, her mother's ghost whispers from beneath a tangle of blackberry briars. *Fire will burn out all the evil, and good green things will live here again.*

Dancy keeps waiting for her mother's ghost to evaporate and the angel to show up and take her place. It usually happens that way, first her mother and then the angel. Sometimes, she actually prefers the angel. There's a loud *crack*, and Dancy looks up to see that the roof has collapsed completely. The sky is lit with a flurry of red-orange cinders as the last of the shadows, freed from the inferno, escape into the night. That's okay. She didn't come for them. Where they go and what they do, that's none of her concern. Someone might almost mistake them for smoke, streaming up and out of the flames. One passes directly over her head and vanishes into the thick wall of live oaks and magnolia behind the little cemetery. The shadow's screaming, so maybe it believes it could die in the fire. Maybe it's even afraid, Dancy thinks, and then she thinks about all the places a shadow can hide.

Those are the souls of bad people, Julia Flammarion assures her daughter. *They were never baptized or they died without making confession, so they can never go to Heaven. Some of them were pagan Indians, and some of them were murderers and thieves and drug addicts.*

Dancy glowers at the blackberry thicket where her mother's hiding, not so sure she believes that God would turn an Indian into one of those shadows just because it never got the chance to be baptized. That sounds even less fair than most things seem to her, but she knows there's no point arguing with her mother.

Dancy glances up at the eastern sky above the tops of the trees, and there's the faintest pink and purple hint of dawn. The heat from the fire is keeping the air around her warm, so at least she doesn't have to worry about the dew or the morning chill. Then she remembers her knife, that she hasn't even cleaned the blade the way the angel has told her she should always do. She looks down at the monster's dark blood already gone to a crust on the steel and frowns. She'll have to find a stream or a pond somewhere to wash it clean, as clean as it's ever going to get. She wipes it once against the leg of her jeans, but hardly any of Elandrion's blood comes off the carving knife.

"Is it over?" Dancy asks her mother. "Do you think that was the last one?"

I ain't the one you ought to be asking that question, her mother replies, then rustles about in the briars like a raccoon or a possum.

"Sometimes I think I'm crazy," Dancy says.

You fight those thoughts, her mother says, sounding angry now. *That ain't nothing but the demons trying to slow you down, trying to confuse you and slow you down.*

"Is that what she was?" Dancy asks her mother. "Elandrion. Was she a demon?"

There's a long silence from the ghost of Julia Flammarion, then, and Dancy sits on the headstone listening to the roar and crackle of the burning church, to the screams of fleeing shadows and the uncomfortable, rustling sounds the trees are making, as if the fire frightens them.

No, her mother says. *You remember what I taught you about the Watchers, the Nephilim?* And Dancy says that yes, she remembers, even though she really only *half* remembers.

There were giants in the earth in those days; and also after that, when the sons of God came in unto the daughters of men, and they bore children unto them.

"So Elandrion, she was one of the Watchers? She was half angel?" Dancy asks and wipes the knife against her pants leg again with no better results than the first time.

They have many other names, her mother says, and then the blackberry thicket grows still and silent.

But the monster told Dancy that she should know better than to believe it had any name at all. She considers telling her mother that it said that, then decides she doesn't need to hear anything more just now about all the ways the evils of the world will try to deceive her.

She touches the tacky bloodstain on her jeans, the small smear the knife's left behind, and suddenly she's back inside the church and the fire hasn't started yet and the monster isn't dead. She's just buried her knife in its throat all the way up to the hilt, and it looks surprised, more surprised than hurt or scared or anything else. Blood that's black as molasses runs from between its sharp yellow teeth. She pulls the knife free and the shadow things howl their disbelief as she raises her arm to plunge it in again, meaning to cut off the monster's head, just like her angel told her she ought to do.

But it's speaking again, strangling on its own blood, but she can make out the words clearly enough. And Dancy's hand hesitates, halfway down to the monster's windpipe.

"Now I see," it says. "Yeah, that's a damn good trick. That's an amazing fucking trick, hiding there in her skin, and I don't think she even *knows*—"

But then the knife comes down again, comes down so hard it goes in all the way to the monster's spine, and Elandrion closes its empty, boiled-egg eyes and doesn't try to say anything else at all. Its body shudders, and Dancy smells smoke, and then the shadows begin to scream—

She opens her eyes, disoriented and almost tumbling off the edge of the headstone, wondering how long it's been since she shut them, if it's only been a moment or an hour. She glances back at the eastern sky, and it's not much brighter than the last time she looked, so it couldn't have been very long. There's an angry sound behind her, and she knows that it's the angel.

"I don't want to do this anymore," she tells it, as though what she wants might actually matter to it. "I've killed three of them now. Find someone else to chase down all the rest. I'm done for."

But she knows better, that there's a long road ahead of her, whether she's had enough or not, and she sits on the headstone and listens to the fire and the panicked cries of the shadow things. But mostly she's listening to what the angel's saying, how she's got to walk east, towards the scalding summer sun, and somewhere out there she'll find a gas station and a hand-painted sign that reads LIVE PANTHER—DEADLY MAN EATER in tall white letters. The angel tells her to kill everything and everyone she finds there, whether it looks like a monster or not.

And she nods her head, because she knows she'll never say no, and it doesn't matter how many monsters she has to kill. Because her mother's told her time and time again about seeing the gates of Hell and all the demons swimming beneath the sea that tried to make sure that she drowned herself. So she knows there are worse things, no matter how tired she might get.

She sits on the headstone for a few more minutes, until the angel is finished talking about the LIVE PANTHER sign and leaves her alone. Then Dancy stands up and slips the scabby knife into the waistband of her jeans. There will be somewhere nearby she can scrub it clean again. She picks up the heavy duffel bag and stares at the blazing ruins of Grace Ebeneezer Baptist Church just a little longer before she leaves the cemetery, careful to shut the squeaky wrought-iron gate behind her, and Dancy Flammarion follows sunrise down Dry Creek Road, just the way her angel said she should.

Highway 97

I.

It's two or three hours past midnight, but still long hours left until dawn, and the albino girl is beginning to get sleepy. She's been walking since sunset, almost always walking at night to avoid the blistering, unblinking white eye of the summer sun, and her shoulder has finally stopped aching and gone numb from the constant weight of her duffel bag and the black umbrella tied onto it. She stops and lets the worn canvas bag, which once belonged to her grandfather, slide off her shoulder and into the weeds and gravel at the side of the road. Even this late, she can still smell the asphalt cooling down and wonders if it'll be hard again before morning and the next day's heat. She can also smell the pine and bald cypress trees pressing in close on either side, and stagnant, swampy water, and her own sweat, and something sickly sweet that she thinks might be magnolia blossoms.

The moon is only a few nights past full, and the sky is filled with the cold white fire of stars, so it's not so very dark, and she glances back the way she's come to see if the shaggy black dog's still following her. It is, still walking right down the middle of the highway on its long legs like dogs never get run over by trucks and cars. If she stands here very long, it'll catch up with her again, and she doesn't want to talk to it anymore, doesn't want to hear the things it has to say. The last couple of miles, it's been singing hymns, mostly "Nearer, My God, to Thee," over and over and over again. Sometimes it gets all the words right, and sometimes it makes up its own words, and some other times it just hums.

It looks up at her, and its eyes flash blue-green.

"Aren't you getting tired yet?" the dog barks. "You aiming to walk all damn night?"

"I walk until it's time to stop," she replies, and the dog snorts.

"Well, I think my paws are bleeding," it sighs. "At this rate, I'm gonna wear them straight on down to the bone and gristle."

"I don't remember anyone asking you to follow me. You can stop anytime you want. I wish you would."

"Why are you in such a goddamned hurry?" the dog asks, and then it makes a smacking, thirsty noise.

"Why are *you* following me?"

"No fair. I asked you first," the dog tells her, and then it trots the last few yards between them to the spot where the albino girl's standing and sits down in the weeds beside her duffel bag.

"That's my business. It ain't none of yours."

"La-dee-fucking-dah," barks the black dog.

The black dog is bigger than any dog she's ever seen before, bigger than a German shepherd or a black and tan coonhound, and it stinks. The girl wrinkles her nose and wonders if it's been rolling in something dead, a roadkill armadillo or a deer or maybe just a possum.

"You smell awful," she says.

"You're not exactly a bushel of roses your own self," the dog snaps back and flares its nostrils, sniffing the air around her. "When *was* the last time you made the acquaintance of a bar of soap?"

"At least I don't smell like rot," she tells the dog and rubs at her shoulder, which has started aching again.

"Don't fool yourself. You reek of death."

"Dogs can't talk," the albino girl says, hoping that will settle matters once and for all, but knowing that it won't. She stares longingly at the eastern sky, wishing for some faint hint of daybreak, a purple-gray smudge of false dawn on the horizon, but there are only the shimmering stars hung above the black silhouette of trees. There's a screech owl calling out in the woods somewhere nearby, a mournful sort of cry like the whinny of a very small horse, a horse so small that fairies could ride it, if she believed in fairies and tiny fairy horses. There's a whippoorwill, too, but it sounds farther away than the owl.

"I can't stand around all night," she says and reaches for the duffel bag, the fraying canvas straps that have worn blisters and calluses on her back and both her shoulders. "I'm wasting time."

"And besides, dogs can't talk," the black dog reminds her and laughs. She's never heard a dog laugh before, and the sound makes the hairs on the back of her neck prick up and sends chill bumps up and down her bare arms.

"Leave me alone," she says and slings the heavy bag back across her left shoulder. "Go home. Or are you some sort of stray?"

"That would mean we had something in common, wouldn't it, if I was a stray?"

"Shut up," she says and starts walking again. "And you stop following me."

"You don't own this road," the dog barks at her.

"People built this road. So this is a road for people, not for dogs."

"I bet there was dogs there *with* them," the black dog says. "I bet there was all sorts of dogs to keep them company and chase away the snakes and bark at night if a bear got too close. So, I figure I got just as much business on this road as you do."

"You stop, or I'll start throwing rocks at you."

The dog laughs again, and she can hear its feet on the pavement, the *snik snik snik* of its long nails on the asphalt.

"I got myself some pretty sharp teeth," the dog says, "if I do say so myself. You probably ought to think about that before you start in chucking rocks." And then the dog clears its throat and begins singing again.

"Though like the wanderer, the sun gone down,
Darkness be over me, my rest a stone.
Yet in my dreams I'd be nearer, my God, to Thee . . ."

The albino girl stops and glares over her right shoulder at the black dog. "Don't you know any other songs?" she asks it. "I'm sick to death of hearing that one."

"Oh, hell. I know lots of songs," the dog replies and licks its muzzle. "But this one's my favorite."

"Stop *following* me," the albino girl tells the dog again, and now she starts walking much faster than before, thinking that perhaps the dog's telling the truth and its paws really are sore and if she walks fast enough it'll give up and leave her alone.

But behind her, its claws are still clicking loudly against the road, and it's already started singing again.

"Nearer, my God, to Thee, nearer to Thee!
Even though it be a cross that raiseth me,
Still all my song shall be, nearer, my God, to Thee."

The albino girl looks down at the road and the scuffed toes of her old boots, and because she doesn't know what else to do, she starts singing along with the black dog.

"There let the way appear, steps unto Heaven;
All that Thou sendest me, in mercy given;
Angels to beckon me nearer, my God, to Thee."

And the sticky, warm south Georgia nighttime and the ebony ribbon of Highway 97 stretches out before her, all tar and perdition and possibility, leading the way east towards sunrise and all the terrible things that are waiting there for her, the things she knows and those she doesn't. Behind the girl, the big black dog begins the next verse of "Nearer, My God, to Thee" and the waning moon slips a little lower in the brilliant star-dabbled sky.

II.

It's almost an hour later when the albino girl finally reaches the crossroads somewhere south of Lake Seminole, and she stops and sits down in the tall weeds where she's dropped her duffel bag and umbrella. She's so tired and hungry and sick to death of listening to the black dog sing the same damn hymn that her head's begun to spin. It would be so easy to shut her eyes and drift off right here at the side of the road, and that's just exactly what she would do, if she weren't afraid the highway patrol or a sheriff's deputy might come along and arrest her for being a vagrant. She's only seen five cars and one pickup truck in the last hour, and two of them were headed west. She stuck out her thumb both times she spotted a pair of headlights coming towards her, but no one stopped. No one in the world stops to take on hitchhikers at three or four or five in the morning, especially not albino hitchhikers with big black singing dogs following them.

Around her, the pine forests and bayous have been replaced by open farmland and sleeping houses. There are a couple of gas stations at the crossroads, and a convenience store, and a bar that's also a hamburger joint, but this late everything's closed up tight. There are streetlights here, too, and they shine like bits of Heaven fallen almost all the way down to earth, star fire hung on silver poles. There's a big kudzu patch across the highway from her, and in the night, it's easy to imagine monstrous, looming things in the silhouette of the leaves and vines wrapped about the limbs of dead and strangled trees. Here a misshapen skull set crookedly on crooked shoulders, there the long fingers of a giant's hand reaching for her, straining to twine itself tight about her feet and drag her away into the darkness where the street lights can't ever reach, where not even the scorch of the midday sun can find her. She would lie there in deadly green cathedrals, and curious raccoons and nervous jackrabbits would watch while the kudzu monster took its time, while it slowly suffocated and gnawed and digested her. In the end, not even her bones and teeth would be left behind.

"Up and at 'em," the black dog barks, and the albino girl jerks awake, startled to see the animal sitting on its shaggy haunches only a foot or two away from her, its long splotched tongue lolling from its jaws.

"What?" she mutters and rubs at her eyes. "What do you want now, dog?"

"This ain't no place to go dozing off, that's what."

"I was just resting my eyes. I wasn't asleep."

"Yeah, well, this ain't no kinda place to go 'resting your eyes,' neither. Trust me. One of those goddamn sixteen wheelers comes roaring by, and maybe the man behind the wheel, he'll be resting his eyes, too, and so maybe he lets his rig drift just an *itty-bitty bit* to the right and—"

"I *wasn't* asleep," the albino girl says again and spits because her mouth tastes like shit.

"I've seen it happen."

The girl yawns and then squints up at the night sky. The stars don't seem as bright as before, not with the glare from the street-lights so close by, but there's still no sign of sunrise. Maybe, she thinks, this night intends to go on forever. Maybe she's wandered off the map somehow, wandered straight off the face of the world, and she'll spend the rest of eternity wandering this endless stretch of road with the black dog at her heels singing "Nearer, My God, to Thee." She wonders if the old carving knife in her duffel bag is sharp enough to kill the black dog.

"You know how much farther it is to Bainbridge?" she asks the dog and combs her white hair with her fingertips.

"Bainbridge? Why the sam hill would you want to go to Bainbridge? Aren't there enough hicks and rednecks around here to suit you, you gotta go looking for someplace where they're all clumped up together?"

"You *don't* know, do you?"

"If I were you, I'd go south, maybe head down to Port St. Joe or Apalachicola. I always wanted to see the Gulf of Mexico. How about it, buttercup? Just you and me?"

"I'm not going back to Florida," the albino girl says and gives up on her hair. "I just come from Florida. I've lived there my whole life."

"Is that so? Well, then, I guess you already seen the Gulf of Mexico lots of times."

"No," she tells the dog. "I've never seen the ocean. My momma told me it's just something God put there to hide the way down to Hell, and she said the water's full of demons and sea serpents and the ghosts of drowned sailors and fishermen and suicides, all waiting for people who don't know any better than to come too close."

The dog cocks its head to one side and stares at her for almost a whole minute without saying anything at all.

"What's wrong with you?" she asks, because it's the longest the black dog's been quiet since it first came bounding out of the woods a little while after dusk and started singing.

"That's just about the dumbest damned thing I ever heard, that's what's wrong. Are you some sort of retard or something?"

"My momma knew about the ocean," the albino girl says, ignoring the retard crack because the dog's just a poor dumb animal. Animals don't have souls, not even dogs that can sing "Nearer, My God, to Thee," so she can't really expect them to know anything about God and Hell and demons.

"You think so?" the dog asks and makes a doubtful sort of face.

"She almost drowned herself off Pensacola Beach. She would have, but an angel came along and saved her from the demons."

And then the black dog gets quiet again and just stares at her.

"Anyway," she says, "I'm going to Bainbridge, or near enough," and she stands up and looks at the crossroads. There's a reflective green-and-silver sign to tell her that if she turns left, she'll wind up on State 310 to Lake Seminole and someplace called Recovery, and if she turns south, instead, she'll be on the Hutchinson Ferry Road to Hannatown. But she doesn't need the sign to tell her to keep following Highway 97 on past this intersection, then past Faceville and all the way to Dry Creek Road, not too far south of the Bainbridge city limits. She knows that much, even if she doesn't know how much farther she has left to go or if the dog's one of those things she's supposed to kill or when the sun's going to stop playing games and decide to come up.

"Then I'm afraid this is where we part company," the dog sighs and gets to its feet. It shakes itself once and sneezes loudly. "Damn goldenrod," it says and licks its wet nose.

"I don't need a dog tagging along," the albino girl tells it without looking away from the highway sign. "Besides, you don't want to go where I gotta go, and you don't wanna see what I'm gonna have to see."

"Well, I'll take your word for it," the dog says. "But it's been a pleasure making your acquaintance, buttercup," and then it pricks its ears and looks quickly over its right shoulder at the kudzu patch. The black dog barks twice, then dashes across the road and vanishes into the wall of vines. The kudzu monster seems to twitch and rustle around for a moment, like it's not so happy about having a talking dog scrounging about inside its belly. And then the night is still again.

And the albino girl is alone.

"Bye, dog," she says and watches the kudzu patch for three or four minutes before she picks up the duffel bag. It feels at least ten pounds heavier than when she set it down, like maybe someone's slipped a small anvil or a pile of rocks in when she wasn't paying attention. If the highway sign's to be believed, there's still three and a half miles left between her and Faceville, and she figures she might make it at least half that far before she gives up and stops and finds some safe, shadowy place to sleep through the long summer day.

"You could have at least told me about the damned dog," she says, just in case the angel's out there listening, just in case it feels like keeping her company for a while. But she isn't very surprised when no one answers. She spares one last look at the kudzu monster, at the spot where the black dog disappeared, and then, because the quiet and the stillness is starting to make her nervous, the albino girl begins to sing as she walks away towards the crossroads and Bainbridge and all the inevitable, awful things she tries not to think too much about. Her voice is thin and tired, worn flat, and there's not a hint of the dog's boisterous delight in the words and the tune, but it's better than nothing at all.

"*Or, if on joyful wing cleaving the sky,*
Sun, moon, and stars forgot, upward I'll fly,
Still all my songs shall be, nearer, my God, to Thee."

Afterword:
On the Road to Jefferson

Author's note: This essay was originally released by Subterranean Press in 2002 as a chapbook to accompany In the Garden of Poisonous Flowers.

I.

"Where do you get your ideas?"

I've been asked that goddamned annoying question so many times in the last few years that I've not only lost count, I've lost *patience.* So, in retaliation, I've about two dozen smart-ass replies to keep at the ready whenever it comes up (and it almost *always* comes up). They range from the Marxist (that's Groucho, not Karl)—"From a little feed shop in Boise. They deliver."—to the stupefyingly subtle—"Um . . ."—to turnabout-is-fair-play tactics—"Where do you get *yours*?" Sometimes body language is best, and the question can be dismissed with a simple shrug or an exasperated rolling of the eyes. Sometimes I pretend I didn't hear what was being asked and just say the first thing that comes to mind, instead. And, honestly, I usually have no clue where I "get an idea." I *don't* get them. They usually just *come* to me, like pimples and troublesome men, without my having invited them. They occur.

But every now and then I can say, *this*, this nasty little thing right *here*. See it? *That's* why I wrote story X or chapter Y. It doesn't happen very often, but it's sort of satisfying in no particular way I can explain when it does happen like that.

In the Garden of Poisonous Flowers is one of those rare stories, rarer still in that it had not one, but two identifiable inspirations. The first is a Dame Darcy illustration (reprinted in the novella) from an issue of her ever-fabulous comic, *Meat Cake*, a wondrously detailed scene of young Victorian women engaged in ghoulish delights, sex, and other mischief in the basement of an old house. An inset shows them armed with shovels and stylish coats, braving a snowy night to rob a grave; we can see the fruits of their labors stretched out on a slab, and some of the women attend the corpse while others attend each other. Yes, well, it's *that* sort of a drawing, and Miss Aramat and the other Ladies of the Stephens Ward Tea League and Society of Resurrectionists owe their existence to that drawing. That's the *first* inspiration.

The second is a little bit more complicated and a whole lot stranger . . .

II.

During my time in Athens, Georgia, way, way back in the midnineties, I did a stint as the vocalist and songwriter for a local goth-folk-blues band called Death's Little Sister. This wasn't long after I'd finished writing *Silk* and it was taking a lot longer to sell than either my agent or I had expected. So I decided I'd be a rock star instead. Luckily, the work for Vertigo came along and the novel did eventually sell, shocking me back to my senses and rescuing me from the indie-rock purgatory that is Athens.

Anyway, one bitterly cold night in November 1996 we played a show at the 40 Watt Club on Washington Street. All our original material, which amounted to about seven or eight songs, plus all our covers—"House of the Rising Sun," "Crimson and Clover," "Sweet Jane," "Bloodletting," and so forth. Enough people showed up that at least it didn't feel like one of our interminable practices, and no one threw anything at us. To make matters worse, someone approached us after the show to ask if we'd like to contribute a track to a compilation of Bowie covers being put together by a local record label. So, we were in pretty good spirits afterwards, which was anything but usual. About one a.m., we loaded out, collected whatever paltry few bucks we had coming from the club, sold a couple of tapes, and then piled into my blue Honda station wagon. All four of us, plus a couple of hangers-on, squished in amongst our gear (amps, a mixing board, mike stands, instruments), elbows in ribs, shoes where shoes ought not be, and our keyboardist sitting in the back-seat floorboard (she was very, very tiny). We had about half a case of truly crappy beer—PBR or Sterling or some such weasel piss—a big bottle of Jägermeister, and another bottle of Wild Turkey, a little weed, and we headed north out of town on I-129.

A pretty bleak stretch of road, leading nowhere any of us had any business going at one o'clock in the morning, half-drunk, stoned, and dressed like a bunch of whores from Hell's cotillion (thank you, Matthew Grasse, wherever you are). To our credit, we *did* have a destination in mind, the old Woodbine Cemetery in Jefferson, about twenty miles north of Athens. At some point, Barry Dillard, our guitarist, had told us a story about a murder-suicide at UGA in 1918 and, he'd said, the murderer was buried in Woodbine. His victim was buried three miles from Woodbine, in a Presbyterian cemetery. I'm sure it has a name, too, but I've forgotten it. And, so the story went, because such stories always go this way, his ghost and the ghost of the woman he killed could be glimpsed at Woodbine from time to time, reunited, wandering aimlessly about the tombstones.

There isn't much between Athens and Jefferson—kudzu, cows, junk cars, house trailers, and "towns" with names like Red Stone, Arcade, Attica, and Clarksboro. Maybe a few state troopers looking for drunken idiots in blue Honda station wagons. Nothing you want to run into on a dark night. And it was a *very* dark night, no moon at all, but not cloudy, either. I remember the sky was clear and the stars were bright, in the way that stars can fill the whole sky, horizon to horizon, and give off no light whatsoever. I remember that someone put in an Echo and the Bunnymen tape and we were halfheartedly singing along. And then, about the time we passed Arcade, one of us spotted a ball of blue-white light, about the size of a football and floating maybe ten feet above the ground, slipping along the side of the highway on our right. There were pine trees along this stretch of road and the ball of light weaved and bobbed along between the trunks.

"Jesus, man, it's Saint Elmo's fire," Barry said. Or maybe that was Mike, our bass player. Someone else said it was a ghost, and I said that it couldn't be because we hadn't even reached the cemetery yet.

We slowed down, and the ball of light slowed down. We sped up, and it sped up. After a mile or so, the novelty began to wear thin and the situation started to get seriously creepy. The girl I'd drafted to drive pulled over to the side of the road just as the pines ended and the land opened up into pasture again. The ball of light floated out of the trees, *turned*, and drifted over a barbed-wire fence, coming to a stop in the middle of the road, maybe ten yards in front of the Honda.

We sat and stared. It bobbed up and down. We sat and stared some more. I don't remember anyone saying much of anything, just Echo and the Bunnymen crooning from the tape deck. The thing above the road made no sound and didn't seem to give *off* light. I recall wondering why we weren't bathed in blue-white light. The road beneath it was perfectly dark.

"Let's just get the fuck out of here," Barry said and, as if the thing had heard him, it dimmed slightly and then began to rise, going straight up, higher and higher until it seemed not much more than a particularly bright star. At some point we finally lost sight of the thing and the driver pulled back onto the I-129, heading for Jefferson.

"I don't think I want to go anymore," Shelly, the keyboardist in the floorboard, said. There was a little nervous laughter and then, "No, I'm serious," she said. "Turn the car around and let's go back to town."

And before we had time to start arguing about whether we were going back to Athens or continuing on to Jefferson to hunt ghosts, there was an *extremely* loud BLAM and the car swerved off the road into a weedy ditch. A few seconds later, once we were sure that none of us were bleeding or unconscious or disemboweled or anything, Barry climbed out one of the windows (his door was jammed shut).

"It's a blowout," he reported. "We blew a tire."

I had a spare, of course. And, of course, it was also flat.

For the next ten minutes, maybe less, we sat there in the car, rubbing at our various scrapes and bruises, drinking the weasel-piss beer and Jägermeister, and debating whether we'd get shot if we went to one of the houses along the road and asked to use the phone. The girl who was driving (she had a name, but none of this was her idea, so I'm not using it) turned on the flashers and declared that we never should have left town in the first place. I don't remember anyone disagreeing with her.

"What if that thing comes back?" Shelly asked anxiously.

"It won't," I said, hoping I was right, and started looking for the bottle of Wild Turkey, which had rolled under the front seat when we went into the ditch.

And that's when the black Monte Carlo came along, heading south towards Athens, away from Jefferson. It only had one headlight and that didn't seem to work very well.

"Thank God," Shelly grumbled, as the big, ugly Chevy glided across the yellow center line and came to a stop directly in front of us. After sitting in the dark, even that one weak headlight seemed blindingly bright.

Mike—whose door wasn't jammed shut—got out of the car, and a very tall, very fat man, a veritable *mountain* of human flesh, climbed out of the Monte Carlo, and the two of them stood staring at the crippled Honda, shaking their heads. The man from the Monte Carlo was wearing a dark suit and a white shirt, a long coat that almost reached the ground, and a derby hat. He had a long beard, which may have been gray. Echo and the Bunnymen weren't singing anymore because we were still sober enough to think the stereo might run down the battery, and the night was so quiet, so still, those of us in the car had no trouble hearing what Mike and the man from the black car were saying. It went something like this:

"Where are you kids headed this late?"

"Nowhere."

"Well, good, because that's the *only* place you're gonna get to with that tire. Don't you think you should change it?"

"Our spare's flat."

"You're kidding?"

"No, sir. Are you going to Athens? If you're going to Athens, maybe you could give one of us a ride back to town."

"I'm not going to Athens. I'm going to Savannah. I'm going to Savannah, and I don't pick up hitchers."

Their breath fogged in the cold, and Mike hugged himself for warmth, though the guy from the Monte Carlo seemed oblivious to the temperature. He scratched his beard and stared at the flat tire.

"You kids been drinking?" he asked.

"A little," Mike lied.

"So it wouldn't do to just sit here until a cop comes along, then, would it?"

"No, sir. We'd really rather not."

"I don't pick up hitchers."

"Yes, sir."

"I'm going to Savannah. I got to make my delivery before morning."

"Yes, sir," Mike said again, and Shelly, who happened to be his girlfriend, mumbled something rude from the back seat.

I opened the bottle of bourbon, took a small drink, coughed, and that's when I noticed two shiny points of light, like cat eyes caught in the beam of a flashlight, that sort of iridescence, but silver. Two points of light, like silver cat eyes watching us from inside the Monte Carlo. I was suddenly very aware of the cold, the Georgia night stretching out around us, and just how far we were from anywhere light and safe and warm.

I took another sip of bourbon.

"Well, I'll tell someone you're out here," the big man said.

"We'd sure appreciate that."

"I'll tell them to send a wrecker."

"Thank you."

"I'd give you a ride, son, but I don't take hitchers. And I gotta be in Savannah."

And then the big man got back into his black Monte Carlo and drove away. As he passed, I swear I saw a second set of the iridescent eyes watching us from the back seat of the Chevrolet. I drank more Wild Turkey, and then Mike was back in the car again, shivering, letting in the cold.

"What the fuck was *that*?" Barry asked him.

"Lock the doors," Mike said.

"Why?" Shelly asked.

"Just lock the goddamned doors!" And we did, because Mike didn't raise his voice very often and I'd *never* heard him sound scared before.

"Did you see that kid in the front seat?" Mike asked, and I didn't say anything about the silver eyes. "Jesus," Mike said, his teeth chattering, and he stared out his window, up at the November sky full of unhelpful stars.

"So, is he sending someone?" Barry asked, though I'm sure he'd heard the big guy from the Monte Carlo as clearly as the rest of us.

"Yeah, man, he's sending someone, okay? He *said* he was sending someone. Hell, I don't know."

"I can't feel my feet anymore," Shelly said, stomping them against the back of the front seat. "I think I'm freezing to death. I think I'm getting hydrophobia."

"You mean *hypothermia*," the girl behind the wheel said. "Hydrophobia is rabies."

"Whatever," Shelly replied and stomped her feet twice as hard. "Jesus, did you fucking *see* that kid?"

"What kid?" Barry asked, and Mike shook his head and shivered.

"The kid sitting right there in the fucking front seat. Jesus."

"I didn't see anyone but the big fucker in the bowler."

"It was a derby," the driver said quietly.

"What's the fucking difference?"

I passed the bottle back to Mike, and he stared at it a moment like maybe he'd forgotten what it was for.

"That dude, man, he smelled like something fucking dead. He smelled like rotten meat."

Barry lit a cigarette then, his face caught for a moment in the yellow-orange glow from his lighter, and no one said much of anything else that I can recall. A few cars passed, heading north or heading south, but no one else stopped to help. In a little while, maybe twenty or thirty minutes, a red tow truck showed up, just like the big guy had promised, and took us all back to town.

III.

I'm forever drawing connections where none exist, or, to be more precise, where many other people would not draw connections, which is another thing entirely.

The hovering ball of blue light.

The blowout.

The strange man from the Monte Carlo.

The silver eyes shining from the dark car.

All these things in the space of fifteen minutes. My mind draws connections, and I'm left to puzzle over their legitimacy.

I don't believe in UFOs, not in the popular sense, anyway, that unidentified flying objects are extraterrestrial spacecraft. I *do* believe in extraterrestrial life, but I know, as a scientist, that the odds of its getting from planet to planet, much less crossing interstellar distances, are remote. Anyway, what we saw that night didn't look like a "spacecraft." I'm entirely willing to entertain the possibility that the blue ball of light was some unusual electrical discharge, though I couldn't begin to imagine what its origin might have been, or why it shone so brightly but didn't seem to *radiate* any light at all. Was it something meteorological? Seismic? Man made? Insects? I have no idea whatsoever. I can only say it was one of the strangest things I've ever seen.

As for the big man in the Monte Carlo, well, one meets strange people on the highway late at night, and sometimes they don't smell so great. It's the silver eyes that still bother me, from time to time. A couple days after the interrupted trip to Jefferson and Woodbine Cemetery, Death's Little Sister got together in the east Athens attic we'd converted into a practice space and, at some point, someone finally mentioned the odd events after the show. I think we'd all been avoiding talking about that night—the light, the Monte Carlo, and its driver— and I don't remember who finally brought it up. I also don't remember who suggested that the silver eyes might have been a dog's eyes, that there might have been a dog in the car with the man, which also might have helped explain the odor. But I do remember how that suggestion upset Mike, and he insisted that there *hadn't* been a dog, just a kid sitting up front, and that there had been something "all wrong" about the kid, but he wouldn't elaborate and we didn't press him.

I think that, all those years later, when I sat down to write the short story that grew into the novella *In the Garden of Poisonous Flowers*, I'd hoped that by burying some of the events of that strange night in fiction I might divest them of at least a modicum of their weirdness. But it doesn't seem to have worked. Lonely country roads still make me nervous now, and they never did before. I watch for lights in the sky more than I once did, and dread the glint of silver eyes from the windows of passing cars.

Caitlín R. Kiernan
9 January 2002
Liberty House, Birmingham

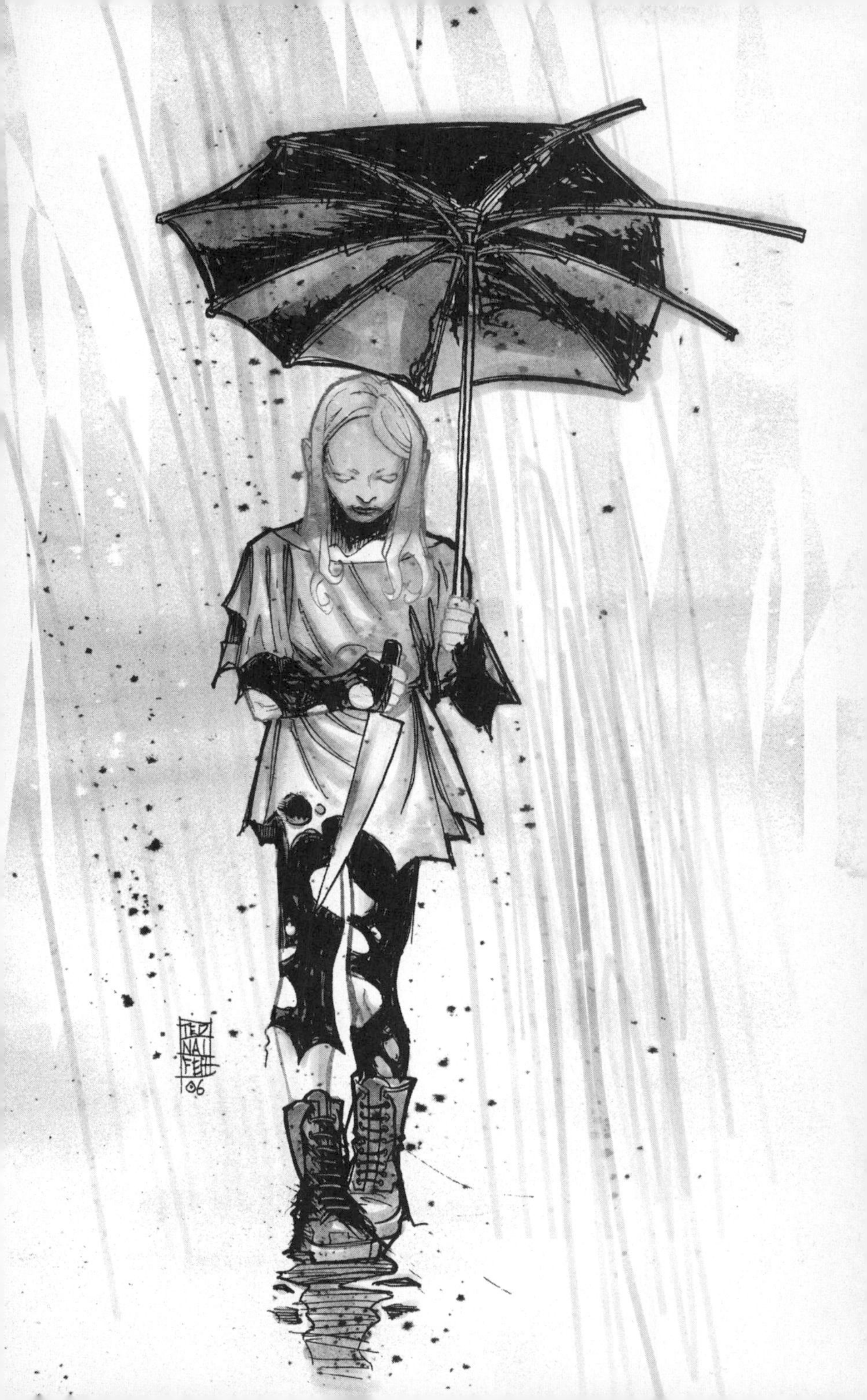
TED
NAI
FEH
'06

Photo courtesy of Kyle Cassidy.

Caitlín R. Kiernan is the author of such critically acclaimed novels as _The Red Tree_ and _The Drowning Girl: A Memoir_ (winner of the James Tiptree, Jr. and Bram Stoker awards, nominated for the Shirley Jackson, Locus, World Fantasy, British Fantasy, Nebula, and Mythopoeic awards). To date, her short fiction has been collected in nine volumes, including _Tales of Pain and Wonder, A Is for Alien_, and _The Ape's Wife and Other Stories_. From 1996 to 2002, she scripted _The Dreaming_ and two _Sandman Presents_ miniseries for DC/Vertigo, then returned to comics in 2012 with _Alabaster: Wolves_. Born in Dublin, Ireland, and raised in the Deep South, she now lives in Providence, Rhode Island.

Also by Caitlín R. Kiernan

Silk
Threshold
Low Red Moon
Murder of Angels
Daughter of Hounds
The Red Tree
The Drowning Girl
The Wide Carnivorous Sky (forthcoming)

From Dark Horse
Alabaster: Wolves
Alabaster: Grimmer Tales (forthcoming)

Writing as Kathleen Tierney
Blood Oranges
Red Delicious
Cherry Bomb (forthcoming)